BISHOP'S KNIGHT
ENDGAME TRILOGY

Katie Reus

Cover art: Jaycee of Sweet 'N Spicy Designs
Editor: Julia Ganis
Author website: https://www.katiereus.com

Publisher's Note: This is a work of fiction. Names, characters, places, and incidents are either the products of the author's imagination or used fictiously, and any resemblance to actual persons, living or dead, or business establishments, organizations or locales is completely coincidental.

Bishop's Knight /Katie Reus. -- 1st ed.
KR Press, LLC

ISBN-13: 9781635561098
ISBN-10: 1635561094

eISBN: 9781635561081

For Kaylea Cross (again). Here's to yet another book you helped me plot during our trip to New Orleans. Thank you.

Praise for the novels of Katie Reus

"Exciting in more ways than one, well-paced and smoothly written, I'd recommend *A Covert Affair* to any romantic suspense reader."
—Harlequin Junkie

"Sexy military romantic suspense." —USA Today

"I could not put this book down. . . . Let me be clear that I am not saying that this was a good book *for* a paranormal genre; it was an excellent romance read, *period.*" —All About Romance

"Reus strikes just the right balance of steamy sexual tension and nail-biting action....This romantic thriller reliably hits every note that fans of the genre will expect." —*Publishers Weekly*

"Prepare yourself for the start of a great new series! . . . I'm excited about reading more about this great group of characters."
—Fresh Fiction

"Wow! This powerful, passionate hero sizzles with sheer deliciousness. I loved every sexy twist of this fun & exhilarating tale. Katie Reus delivers!" —Carolyn Crane, RITA award winning author

"A sexy, well-crafted paranormal romance that succeeds with smart characters and creative world building."—Kirkus Reviews

"*Mating Instinct*'s romance is taut and passionate . . . Katie Reus's newest installment in her Moon Shifter series will leave readers breathless!"
—Stephanie Tyler, *New York Times* bestselling author

Fifteen months ago

Evie slowly circulated around the dimly lit bar, adrenaline pumping through her. Tonight was the night her special ops CIA team ended their three-month operation. Yerik Morozov, the man her team was looking for, was supposed to be at this club for his birthday.

Morozov ran the Morozov mafia in a midsized Russian-Ukraine border town. He'd taken over the organization from his father—who had been brutal, but much smarter than his son.

Evie's team was here to take him out. He'd started selling weapons to an Iranian terrorist group. He hadn't even been on the CIA's radar before, but now he was a problem and they were going to take him out before his group and reach grew too powerful to squash.

She and Samara—wearing disguises and using aliases—had been coming to this club for the last two weeks, drinking, dancing, partying it up, flirting with low-level Morozov thugs. She was posing as a rich socialite from another province, and Samara was also a rich socialite from Australia here visiting.

Tonight she wore the same wig she'd been donning the last couple weeks—a waterfall of platinum blonde hair falling down to her butt—bright green contacts, and her cheeks were fuller thanks to subtle stage makeup. She preferred blonde wigs because they were such a contrast to her real jet-black hair but still went well with her coloring.

As she reached the bar, a regular who did low-level grunt work for the Morozov family smiled at her. "Lena," he said, clearly pleased to see her.

She smiled before pouting ever so subtly and answering in Russian. "Maxim, tell me I'm not going to have to buy my own drinks tonight."

His gaze fell to her glossy, red-slicked lips before he motioned to the bartender.

"I can't believe my gender," her team leader, Luca, said through her earpiece, his tone disgusted. "So pathetic."

Samara snickered in agreement over the comm line but Evie kept her smile in place, nodding politely at the bartender who placed a glass tumbler in front of her. The bartender—Arman—worked for the Morozov crew against his will. He loathed them since they'd kidnapped his cousin and forced her to work in one of their brothels. Now Arman had to pay them "protection money." Turning him hadn't been hard. He was risking everything to help them out and she was going to make sure he got out of here alive.

As Maxim started talking to the bartender, Evie reached into her envelope clutch and pulled out a small, circular incendiary device, quickly securing it to the bottom of the bar.

Samara was doing the same on one of the other bars across the expansive dance floor. Even though they'd been coming in here for weeks, they had come in separately, not as friends. They'd talked before, under the guise of polite chitchat when at the same table with any of the Morozov thugs, but they didn't associate with each other outside this club.

Everyone on this op had a role to play and she was ready to do her part. Ready to kill Yerik Morozov.

The leader for this op was Luca Ramos, though he was actually in play, not in the operation van two blocks away with Ben and Seamus. Ben loved his role in the command center, but Seamus was pissed that he'd been sidelined for this op. Since he'd tangled with one of Morozov's recently promoted lieutenants, they couldn't risk him blowing their cover.

As Maxim blew cigarette smoke in her direction, she subtly waved it away.

"So what's it going to take to get you to go out with me?" He played his fingers up her bare arm, but not any farther than her elbow thankfully.

She lifted an eyebrow, challenging him. "You've still got to impress me." Grinning, she took a sip of the drink, swallowing most of it down in two gulps. She was very good at playing the tipsy party girl. Thanks to Arman's sleight of hand, it was soda water with lime on the side, not vodka and tonic.

"He's here," Samara said into her earpiece. "Target in my sight."

Hell yeah. It was go time. "How about you take me out tomorrow in that car you keep bragging about?" Evie asked as she slid off her barstool, walking her fingers up his chest.

Maxim straightened and nodded. "Where should I pick you up?"

"I'll text you later. I see someone I know." She blew him an air kiss as she stepped away, sure he was watching her ass while she walked.

The loud music—some kind of techno crap— thumped around them. Purple and blue lights flashed in beat with the music, giving her a low-grade headache. She reminded herself why she loved her job, that she was making a difference by ridding the world of people who wanted to see it burn.

Swaying with the music, Evie smoothly shifted through a group of dancing women, only making brief eye contact with Samara and a local woman, Daria, who they'd also recruited. Daria was a waitress at the club and had lost a sister to this group. She was more than willing to help out even though she was risking her life the same as Arman.

Even though the Morozov mafia's reach was hurting Evie's own country, hurting many innocent people around the globe, she wanted to destroy them for the way they'd hurt this town alone. They were leeches, sucking out the life force of everything around them. And Morozov was from here, hurting his own people. It was revolting.

Daria approached, wearing a teeny blue sparkly dress and carrying a tray of shots. "He's got two of his lieutenants with him. Seven men total, all armed. Ivan is in there." She dropped the information so smoothly, dancing to the music and carrying the tray without spilling anything. "This one," she said pushing one of the shots out.

Evie took the shot of water and tossed it back. Then she dropped a bill on the tray. "Thank you. Make sure you've exited out the back in the next ten minutes."

Daria nodded and made her way across the dance floor, offering up shots as Evie crossed to the roped-off VIP section. She lifted an eyebrow as the beefy security guy eyed her, not removing the rope. Instead he crossed his arms over his chest, watching her with cold blue eyes. He'd asked her out weeks ago and she'd turned him down flat.

Before she could snap something haughty at him, Ivan—a man she'd been flirting with the last couple weeks—called out an order to let her through.

She sniffed in annoyance and flipped her hair over her shoulder as he lifted the rope. Samara and a few other club girls were right behind her, but she didn't look in her teammates' direction.

"Lena." Ivan, an affable guy—for a gangster—waved her over from his seat around a circular table with others she recognized. Including Yerik Morozov.

Ivan was much higher up the food chain than Maxim—who wasn't even allowed past the velvet rope. Ivan was a special kind of garbage. He ran two of the local brothels, though you'd never know it from his charm and attitude. But she'd seen the pictures of what he'd done to some of the women who'd tried to run away. And Evie was going to make sure he died too. It wasn't part of the op, but it was necessary.

She smiled widely as he pulled her into his lap, all the while fighting the instinctive cringe at having his arms wrapped around her.

He turned to Yerik. "This is the girl I was telling you about. She is beautiful, yes?"

Yerik looked her up and down, nodding as if he was inspecting a piece of meat, before he turned away from her. She was a little older than he liked—in her late twenties. His gaze narrowed on Samara with interest as she approached the table with a few of the other girls, most of whom were here of their own accord.

Evie patted Ivan's face gently, making him laugh lightly. "We need vodka."

"Grab us a tray of drinks!" he ordered one of the security guys.

"Get ready," Luca said in her ear. "As soon as he drinks, start moving toward the exit."

Evie knew what to do. So did Samara. But Luca was a steady presence in her ear, reminding her that he, Ben and Seamus had their backs if things went haywire. They'd worked a number of ops together and she respected all of them.

This was all part of their plan. "So what are we celebrating tonight?" She indicated the two empty bottles of champagne on the table as the security guy returned with a tray of vodka shots. She knew exactly which shot Yerik needed to drink.

Her heart rate increased. This was it.

"It is my boss's birthday," Ivan said, motioning to Yerik.

"Oh, birthday boy." Smiling, she picked up two shot glasses, one for herself and one for the man who needed to die. "I'll drink to that."

As Yerik took the shot glass, he looked at her, amusement glinting in his pale, calculating eyes—probably thinking about how much money he could make off her if he put her to work in one of his brothels. The custom-made suit and expensive Italian shoes couldn't hide what kind of scum he was. "I would like more than just a drink."

"If you're a good boy, I'll dance for you." She wiggled against Ivan's lap, making him laugh uproariously, even as she clinked her shot glass to Yerik's. "To the birthday boy." Then she tossed her shot back, praying he did the same. His security had proved to be decent, making poison the best way to get to him. In the time she'd been coming here, no one had thought to check drinks—likely because they trusted that the owner was too afraid of them. And she was a silly woman after all; she doubted they would suspect her.

Yerik tossed his back as well and all his men did the same, toasting his birthday. He was all about excess in everything. Drinks, women, drugs. And he was about to die at the age of thirty-nine. *Good riddance.*

He patted his knee. "Where is my dance?"

She playfully kissed Ivan once on the cheek before standing, ready to straddle this piece of garbage and dance for him for as long as she had to. But he started choking on air.

Yes.

Yerik grasped at his throat, clawing at the invisible fingers choking the life out of him. "Can't...breathe..."

Ivan practically shoved her out of the way as he and the others closed in on Yerik.

Evie slowly moved toward the exit with Samara as panic in the little VIP area spread.

"Oh my God!" one of the women cried, stumbling in her stilettos. "Is he dead?"

"Poison," Ivan snapped out, rage in his voice as Yerik started foaming at the mouth.

A thick, meaty hand wrapped around Evie's upper arm as she reached the roped-off exit.

"You're not going anywhere," the thug snapped at her, digging his fingers into her arm.

"Get out of there," Luca said in her earpiece. "Now!"

"You don't have to be so rough!" she snapped, giving a weak pull against him.

"Her! She gave him the shot." One of the men pointed at her, shoving the table out of the way as he barreled toward her.

Evie looked around in confusion, acting as if she was surprised by their anger.

Next to her Samara slid her hand into her clutch and—boom!

An explosion ripped through the air as one of the incendiary devices exploded.

The man's grip on her loosened. Evie was ready for it, already jumping into action. She reared back with her elbow, slamming it into the guard's face even as she shoved past him, sprinting with Samara toward the crowd of running people.

This wasn't exactly how tonight was supposed to go—they were supposed to have been out of the VIP section before shit blew up. It would have been a hell of a lot easier to blend in that way. But this was doable. Heart racing, she and Samara shoved people out of the way, trying to blend in.

A hail of bullets exploded from the VIP section. Glass shattered above them as the lights were destroyed. People screamed in horror.

Evie reached into her own purse and set off another device. These wouldn't hurt anyone, simply create smoke and chaos. Something in abundance right now, but more would definitely help.

There were too many people, the panic too much, the crowd too thick as everyone ran for the main exit.

"Behind the bar!" Evie shouted over the din of gunfire and screams.

The flashing lights and music continued thumping as she veered off from the crowd.

Evie ran in her kitten heels, grasping the front of the metal bar top and propelling herself over it like a hurdle. She rolled into the back of the bar, grunting from the impact, but ignored the flash of pain.

Samara tumbled down beside her, expression tense as they both reached for the weapons strapped underneath the interior of the bar. Arman was hopefully long gone, but he'd come through with the backup.

She pulled out two pistols as Samara did the same.

Bottles exploded above them, bits of glass falling into her blonde wig.

"You guys hit?" Luca shouted through the earpiece.

"We're good," Samara answered.

"Get ready to run."

"Meet at the rally point," Ben said. "We're already en route. We'll pick you guys up."

Evie nodded, though no one could see her. Taking a deep breath, she prepared to move from her cover and return fire as Luca counted down. "Three, two, go!"

Two simultaneous explosions ripped through the air.

Evie and Samara jumped up at the same time, weapons raised.

Evie pulled the trigger, firing at the nearest target. A hole had been blasted through the opposite bar as well as the roof above the VIP section.

Bodies were everywhere, Yerik's men either dead or crying out in pain.

"At your three o'clock," Samara snapped.

Evie swiveled, fired again even as they ran toward the exit. She hit her mark—Ivan's center mass. He wasn't getting up from that.

Bullets whizzed past her head as they dove, taking cover behind a fallen high-top table.

Two bullets ripped through it, missing her head by inches.

She lifted her arm, blindly firing.

"You've got an opening," Luca shouted.

They both jumped up, firing back a spray of bullets as they raced for the exit. Only ten yards to go.

Yerik's men would have called reinforcements by now so they had maybe thirty seconds to get to the getaway car. Less than a minute after that, they would get into their backup vehicle.

Luca stepped out from behind one of the oversized speakers by the DJ booth, an AR-15 raised. "Run!"

Evie and Samara sprinted the last few feet for the exit door as the sound of more gunfire filled the club.

"There." Relief punched through her to see Ben's vehicle idling across the street. Everyone else had scattered, racing down the sidewalk, far away from the chaos of smoke and gunfire.

"Go, go, go!" Luca was behind them, tossing a grenade through the doorway as he followed them.

Heat licked against her back as they dove into the vehicle. Evie winced as her shoulder slammed into the hard metal of the van's floor, then again as Samara landed on top of her.

"Get your ass off me," she groaned.

"Anyone hit?" Seamus asked from the driver's seat, concern in his voice.

Once they all confirmed they were fine, Evie asked, "Any civilian casualties?"

Ben, sitting in the front passenger seat, didn't look up from his tablet. "None that I know of yet. I'm scanning the police radios and hospitals for more information."

She gritted her teeth, breathing in and out as they took a sharp turn. They'd be close to the second getaway vehicle now. "Things shouldn't have gone so volatile so quickly."

Luca just grunted, shrugging one of his big shoulders. A large man at well over six feet, he was military trained and always so calm in every operation. He was who she wanted to emulate. "That's why we prepare for the worst but hope for the best."

She nodded as the van jerked to a halt in the nearly full parking lot. Ripping off her wig, she exited with the others as they all made their way to their respective vehicles, splitting up into different directions. Within half an hour, they'd all meet at the rally point. Unless anything went wrong.

Which was always a possibility. But they hadn't had a tail so they should be good.

Her heartbeat was still erratic even as she pulled onto the street, keeping her driving smooth as she passed a police car with blaring sirens and flashing lights going in the opposite direction.

Tonight she'd expected to poison Yerik, and have some infighting and confusion among the group. Sure, she'd been the one to give him the poison. But she was just a club girl. They'd reacted much quicker than any of them had expected.

Luca was right—this was why they prepared for the worst. Of course her boss was going to be pissed about the shooting at the club, but some things were unavoidable.

And Yerik was dead. That was what mattered.

Sometimes she worked in shades of gray, and while she didn't always like it, she understood the greater good. When she'd first started working for the CIA she hadn't been sure she could do the job.

But at the end of the day, she knew she made the world a better place. That a whole lot of people were alive and free because of her. And she slept fine at night.

* * *

Evie popped the top off the beer Luca handed her as she joined him and the others around the table of their safe house the next day. "News?" she asked, looking at Ben.

"No civilian deaths. A few injuries from gunshots, but mainly people who got trampled in their escape. Yerik is dead and so are most of his guys, including Ivan." He said Ivan's name in disgust. "The brothels have been disbanded as there's no one in charge. I talked to Arman and he and Daria are both safe. He's heading north with his cousin."

Evie was glad for the confirmation of Ivan's death. At her hand—and she wouldn't suffer any guilt because of it.

He continued, looking at his tablet. "Another local gang is taking advantage and going to war with the rest of the Morozov crew. They're not going to be a problem anymore. Not with so much infighting. They'll wipe each other out."

"Good." Samara's tone was savage.

"And…we've all been called to Miami." Ben looked at Evie as he spoke.

She blinked in surprise. "Miami?" It was her hometown and somewhere she never, ever worked.

"Yep. We're going to be teaming up with the Feds for an op. And you're going to be playing the role of a lifetime—yourself."

"Details?"

"None yet. I just know it's being called the Jensen op."

CHAPTER ONE

Present day

Evangeline Bishop stripped off her boxing gloves when she heard her phone buzzing across the bench. She'd been in Miami for a month and the shit had already hit the fan. In more ways than one.

After an insane day, she'd needed a break from simply sitting in the hospital waiting room for news she wasn't sure was ever coming. And a quick thirty-minute workout that included pounding on the giant punching bag in her brother Ellis's extra room had helped clear her head some.

Her parents wanted her to move into their home until she found a place of her own, and as tempting as living on her parents' giant estate sounded, she knew she'd go crazy within twenty-four hours, so she'd opted to live at her brother's place.

Wasn't like he was using it right now. No, because Ellis was in hiding somewhere, wanted for murdering one of his partners with the DEA. He'd been charged with the crime over a week ago and had gone on the run. Something she couldn't wrap her head around. She knew he hadn't done it—there was no way in hell her Boy Scout middle brother would have done it, and if he had, he wouldn't have gotten freaking caught. But the jackass had gone to ground and hadn't reached out to any of them.

Her oldest brother... She couldn't even think about Evan right now. She'd been at the hospital four hours earlier and had planned to stay, but her brother's fiancée and her parents had promised they wouldn't leave. And if she was honest with herself, getting out of there for even just a bit had helped her focus. He'd been in a medically induced coma for three weeks and so far it didn't look like that was changing.

When she glanced at the number on screen, she didn't recognize it, but not many people had this particular cell phone number.

She frowned as she read the text message. *I'm on the back porch. Don't shoot.*

Who the hell is this? she typed back.

Samara.

She blinked in surprise but still grabbed the pistol she'd placed underneath the bench in the middle of a stack of towels.

She wasn't expecting a threat here but some habits she'd take to her grave. Not to mention that one of her brothers had been set up for murder. And whoever had done it would pay. No doubt about that. Whenever she figured out who that someone was, of course. So it wasn't out of the realm of possibility that someone might come here looking for Ellis—though she kind of doubted it. Because how big of a dumbass would he be to show up at his own home? Besides, it would be even dumber to text her an alert.

Pistol at her side, she jogged down the stairs, keeping all the lights off. Her eyes adjusted to the dark quickly.

She turned off the alarm by the front door and made her way to the kitchen, pulling up the video surveillance app on her phone. On the live view, she saw a petite person wearing a hood pulled down over their face hovering by some hydrangea bushes lining the back porch. They were just out of the way of the motion detector, which explained why they hadn't triggered it.

She texted as she walked. *If this is Samara, what's your favorite ice cream flavor?*

She watched the figure type back on their phone. *Ice cream is stupid. Open the damn door.*

She grinned, convinced this had to be Samara. But that didn't mean this wasn't a trap. She flipped on the lights to the back patio and pulled the door open, weapon up.

When Samara stepped forward, her hoodie falling back slightly, Evie quickly tucked her weapon in the back of her workout pants. Then froze when she saw Samara clutching her hip, a crimson line of blood dripping down her fingers and onto the stone steps.

"It's not as bad as it looks," Samara rasped out, her face pale.

Evie covered the distance between them in seconds and wrapped her arm around her friend's shoulders. "Shot or stabbed?" she asked as she helped her up the short set of stairs to the door.

"Shot. And I don't know who did it. But I think I know what it's related to."

"Come on." She guided her friend inside. As soon as she shut the door behind her, she locked it and was already resetting the alarm using her phone's app.

If someone wanted in the house, they were getting inside no matter what. But the alarm would give her a heads-up. Of course that was if they didn't hack the system. It was top-notch, but she never depended on anything to be completely secure. Always have a backup for your backup, was her motto. Plan A, B, all the way to Z.

"Water," Samara said as Evie led her into the pristine kitchen.

Evie left her standing by the center island as she quickly poured her a glass of water. "I think I know the answer, but should I call an ambulance?"

Samara shook her head, her dark ponytail swishing softly. "No."

"You on a job?" Evie asked even as she mentally ran through the list of people she could call for help. If she'd been back in Virginia or DC, the list wasn't exactly long but she had a handful of people she could reach out to. Here in Miami, her options were more limited. She'd retired from the CIA months ago and didn't have many assets here.

"No. I came to see you. Then this happened."

"Let me see," she said.

Wincing, Samara lifted her hand so Evie peeled away the pathetic piece of towel and duct tape to reveal the wound on her hip. Her pants were ripped and the

skin had been torn away, but she wasn't bleeding pro-
fusely. And…the bullet was lodged in her for certain.
No exit wound and hell, she could see the bulge.

"I don't think it went very deep," Samara said, swaying softly.

"Were you followed here?" Evie asked as she rum-
maged inside the pantry for a first aid kit.

"Not sure."

She tucked the kit under one arm. Under different
circumstances she might have attempted to take the
bullet out herself, but if Samara had been followed, she
needed to get her friend somewhere safe. Then get this
damn bullet out. "All right. Let me patch you up, then I
know somewhere we can go." Evie knelt down in front
of her. "Conserve your energy unless there's something
critical you have to tell me right now."

Samara grunted in pain as Evie peeled away the rest
of the duct tape. "This might have something to do
with the Jensen job," her friend rasped out. "I can't be
certain though. But two people involved in that op are
dead."

That was the first Evie had heard. She filed the info
away even as she poured vodka over her friend's
wound. Samara hissed out a curse, but barely moved
otherwise.

"Sorry about this," Evie muttered as she covered the
wound and taped her up. It would have to do for now.
"So why didn't you call me? Why just show up here?"

"I was in Orlando when I got the news about the last
murder from someone on the op. It's a short drive, so I

decided to come see you in person. And I did try your cell phone. Half a dozen times. It kept going to voicemail. I thought maybe... I was hoping you were all right."

Shit. "I had it turned off at the hospital. You didn't leave a voicemail?"

"No. Didn't want a trail."

"How did you know I was here?" Evie wrapped her arm around Samara and helped her walk toward the door that led to the garage.

"Process of elimination. I knew you wouldn't be at your parents'." She snorted at that. "Your 'wanted for murder' brother's house was a good place to start." She hissed in another breath as they stepped down into the garage.

"No more talking." It didn't take long to get Samara into her Mercedes GT. The two-door sports car had been a ridiculous gift from her parents, but right now she was grateful for the speed as she tore out of the driveway.

Just in case Samara had been followed, she took a few detours before heading to the last place she wanted to go. To the last man she wanted to see.

"Star Island?" Samara murmured as she took her final turn.

Star Island was a private neighborhood in South Beach where the über-wealthy lived—including celebrities. But they weren't going to see a celebrity. "Yep. Now hush. You need to save your strength."

Samara completely ignored her. "Please tell me we're not going where I think we are."

"I can tell you that if you want me to lie."

Samara groaned. "What the hell? You think your ex is gonna, what? Help you and your random friend right now? How do you even know he's home?"

"He's home." Or she was pretty certain he was.

"Are you stalking him?"

"I'm not stalking him. I just sort of keep tabs on him."

"Yeah, there's a word for that. It's called *stalking*."

"That's enough. Now for the love of all that is holy, be quiet." She zoomed up to the security gate and pressed the buzzer, knowing whoever was on the other side of that camera could see her clearly. She probably should have called Dylan first but he was a man who kept a tight schedule. And it was Thursday night. He would be home working his ass off like usual. As far as she knew he wasn't seeing anyone, so hopefully he was alone. Ugh. She didn't even want to think about him sleeping with someone else.

His head of security, Leo Webster, answered, his tone icy. Once upon a time he'd been warm and friendly to her. "Ms. Bishop. Is there anything I can help you with?"

"I need to see Dylan. It's an emergency."

Less than ten seconds later, the gate swung open, smooth and soundless. *Damn. Okay, then.* He hadn't even made her wait or beg for entrance. Which...after the way things had ended between them, she'd kind of been expecting him to turn her away.

Evie revved the engine, speeding up the long driveway, and parked under the porte cochere.

Before she'd even rounded the vehicle to help Samara out, Dylan was striding out of the massive front doors that cost more than some people made in a year, wearing dress slacks and a button-down, definitely custom-made Gucci shirt. She was annoyed she even knew that.

"My friend has been shot," she said before he could ask anything. But it was clear she'd surprised him if the slight hitch in his step was any indication. "I can't call the police or go to a hospital—and you've got Finn Kelly on your payroll." His on-call concierge doctor who charged a crap ton for his discreet services. "And I also know this is a huge favor to ask, but can you ask him for help? I'll pay his fees. I just...can't report this gunshot to the police."

His expression was dark as he looked her over once. She ignored the pang in her chest at the sight of him. She had no clue what he was thinking—maybe how much he hated her. But he opened the door anyway and helped her friend out, scooping Samara up into his arms.

"Watch my ass," Samara blurted.

"You didn't get shot in the ass," she muttered. "Even if you're a pain in mine."

"Right back at you. I'm Samara, by the way," she said to Dylan.

"Dylan Blackwood." He kept walking through the foyer.

"I know who you are," her friend said as they all strode into his gigantic kitchen. Everything was practically sparkling.

Dylan lifted an eyebrow but didn't respond otherwise as he stretched Samara out on her side on the center island. "Do you know what kind of ammunition was used?"

"Pistol, standard ammo, I'm guessing. Not hollowpoint that's for damn sure."

He nodded once, then disappeared out of the kitchen and came back less than two minutes later with a small bag in hand. "Finn is on the way but he's about forty-five minutes out. If I can, I'll take the bullet out, but he'll need to stitch you up."

Evie watched him work, his movements quick and methodical. He had limited medical knowledge from his time spent in too many war zones during his years in the military. Samara was quiet as he worked, staring up at the ceiling until he put on steri-strips to close her torn flesh. Then she finally shoved out a hard breath.

"Finn might have to do layered stitches, but for now you'll be okay." He handed Samara a couple codeine and a glass of water.

"Thank you for this." Evie helped Samara to sit up. She still needed answers from her friend, but she wasn't going to ask anything else now. Not until they were alone.

Whatever adrenaline Samara had been experiencing before had faded and now she was clearly exhausted and barely keeping her eyes open.

"Let's get her somewhere more comfortable," Dylan said, practically reading her mind as he lifted Samara up again.

"I could get used to this," Samara murmured, her eyes drifting shut as she rested her head on his sturdy shoulder.

A whole lot of regret knifed through Evie as she remembered all the times she'd been snuggled up in his arms.

Evie walked with him, her strides sure as they made their way through his palatial mansion. She'd been here many times before but never under these circumstances.

"Are you in trouble?" Dylan asked her as they reached one of the guest rooms. She'd been in this room before and thought of it as the "hibiscus room" because there were two giant hibiscus bushes outside one of the windows.

"Maybe." She wasn't sure yet. Samara had mentioned the Jensen job but that was long over. And Jensen had been killed in jail, the sick freak. So...she wasn't sure what her friend had been talking about. She was going to find out though. Especially since the Jensen job was the entire reason she and Dylan had been thrown together—even if he had no clue about that.

"Go easy on her. She misses your ass," Samara slurred as he stretched her out on the bed.

Oh, hell, Samara needed to shut up with that. "Do we need to keep her awake?" Evie asked, ignoring her friend's comment and hoping he would too.

Dylan glanced at his watch. "Finn should be here soon enough."

Sighing, Evie pulled up a chair and sat next to the bed. She still had on her workout gear: tight black pants, a tank top and her silly rainbow-colored sneakers she loved—because Dylan had bought them for her.

Dylan strode to the floor-to-ceiling windows, glancing out at the pool and ocean beyond. It was hard not to sneak a peek at him. His dark hair was cropped close to his head and he had more than a little five o'clock shadow that, of course, made him look even sexier. He was looking away so she couldn't see his dark green eyes, but that didn't matter. She had his face, his expressions memorized. He stood a little over six feet and was well-built, having honed that body with disciplined running and swimming. Damn, the man loved to swim. And she used to love watching him slice through the water.

When he turned toward her, she glanced away, embarrassed at having been caught staring.

"I've got questions," he murmured.

"I know." She didn't look at him again. Couldn't. She didn't want to see anger or hatred on his face. Despite what he might think, she wasn't a robot. She had a heart and it beat for him.

She heard his phone buzz, then a moment later he said, "Finn is here."

Evie counted down in her head how long it took Finn to arrive, knowing that as soon as the doctor did, she'd be forced to be alone with Dylan. Forty-six seconds later, the doctor strode into the room like he owned it.

"What've you got for me?" Finn barely nodded at Dylan or Evie, simply moved to the side of the bed, motioning for Evie to get out of his way.

Without a word, she did, coming to stand by Dylan. When she inhaled that wild, masculine scent that reminded her of the ocean, it was like being sucker punched. She swallowed hard, shoved all the memories she shared with him back in that little box she kept in the darkest, tiniest part of her mind. The part she refused to acknowledge.

"I took the bullet out and gave her codeine like you said. Saved the bullet if you need it." Dylan's voice was steady as he talked to the doctor. "As far as I know she doesn't have any other injuries."

"I don't." Samara's eyes opened, narrowing on the doctor in suspicion.

"Good. You two get out, then. Let me work on my patient."

"Will he call the cops?" Samara asked Dylan.

"I'm not calling the cops." Finn sounded more insulted than anything, which soothed Evie's frayed edges. "Now go."

She wanted to stay, but simply nodded and stepped outside with Dylan. "You trust him?" she asked as he shut the door behind them.

"More than I trust you."

She blinked once, but kept her expression neutral. "That's fair." And she deserved the dig. "Thank you for this."

"Don't do that."

"Do what?"

"Talk to me like we're fucking strangers. Like you didn't just bring a shot woman to my doorstep after not talking to me for six months. Like we haven't fucked in damn near every room in this house."

"What do you want me to say, then? I *am* grateful for this." She'd had no one else to turn to. Her family was in absolute turmoil right now, and then Samara had shown up shot on her doorstep. And no matter what had happened, she still trusted Dylan to have her back.

Dylan's jaw tightened, his green eyes sparking fire as he seemed to rein in his anger. "I want you to tell me why the hell you walked out on me after I proposed."

CHAPTER TWO

One year ago

*E*vie thought she had mentally prepared herself for tonight, but as her mother introduced her to Dylan Blackwood—officially—electricity sparked between them, as
sharp and sizzling as if she'd been shocked. And she was one
hundred percent certain that she was not the only one who
experienced the strange little jolt as they shook hands.

Blackwood's dark green eyes—which had looked so cold
in the surveillance photos her team had recently taken—
showed a clear, male interest in her.

Which was sort of the point of this evening. With no
other choice, she'd broken all her rules and used her family
connections to get an introduction to someone. For her up-
coming op she would be going in as herself, using her real
name and background. Something else she had never done on
a job. But this one called for it, and the location was in her
family's backyard. So here she was, in Miami, getting an introduction to her parents' family friend.

She had to finagle a date out of the very sexy Dylan
Blackwood—and then another date. She needed access to a
certain party, and while she could have gotten an invitation
on her own, Blackwood actually knew the person she wanted
to be introduced to. It wouldn't arouse suspicion if he introduced her to someone and then she later reached out to the
guy. Sometimes the simplest route was the best one.

Even so, she had not expected this strange connection.

"It's a pleasure to see you again." His voice was butter smooth, wrapping around her like a silky caress and sending heat to places that had no business getting all warmed up.

Her lady parts needed to keep themselves under control, thank you very much. "Again?"

His full lips quirked upward. "The last time I saw you, I think you were maybe fourteen or fifteen. It was a god-awful party at my parents' estate and you accidentally knocked over one of their sculptures."

Evie should probably be embarrassed, but a laugh escaped. "Is it terrible that I forgot I did that until just now?"

"If I remember correctly, you barely seemed to notice doing it then."

Her cheeks flushed. "At that age I was only interested in books, video games, and my friends. And soccer. I was probably a little shit about what I did." God, she'd been kind of an ass as a teenager. Even remembering the put-upon attitude she'd had toward her parents—who had given her everything—now made her wince in embarrassment. Her parents had made her and her brothers go to all sorts of soirees that none of them had wanted to attend. But still, she'd been an ass about some things when her parents had given her literally the world. She hadn't appreciated the privilege she'd had until she'd been older.

"You don't remember me, do you?" he asked.

"Kind of," she said. But fourteen-year-old her hadn't noticed him at all back then. Though she was surprised she didn't remember him more because the man was seriously fine. "But you seemed sort of ancient to me."

He laughed, the sound rich and throaty, and hot damn, her lady parts were getting all worked up again. "That's fair. I must have been...around twenty-two then. Definitely an old man compared to you."

She found herself smiling at him, and she wasn't faking it either. "Totally. You were still in the military then, right?"

His expression sobered just a little as he nodded. "Yep. Got out not too long after that."

"And now you're taking over the real estate world, huh?"

"Something like that. So your mom tells me you're back in Miami?"

"For now." As soon as this job was done, she'd be leaving again, but she sure as hell couldn't tell him that. The rest of the world thought she worked for a nonprofit organization. And right now she was currently in Miami supposedly schmoozing with various donors for it. Her cover was solid. Hell, even her parents thought that was her real career.

"Well, I'm glad I didn't blow off this cocktail party," he said.

Oh, there was no mistaking that heated glint in his eyes now. He was a man who knew what he wanted and went after it. And for the first time in her career, she had a feeling she was going to wind up regretting what she was about to do.

* * *

Evie forced herself back to the present as she stared at Dylan, who was expecting an answer. "Can we talk somewhere else? Your office, maybe?" She didn't want to have this conversation outside Samara's bedroom.

He nodded once and motioned for her to follow him, though she knew exactly where his office was.

"How's your brother? Ah, Evan?" he asked, surprising her. "I've been following the news the last few weeks."

The personal question caused her thought process to stutter. "Still in a medically induced coma." The doctors were hopeful he would pull out of it, but for now she wasn't letting herself think too deeply on what would happen if he didn't. Because she could *not* imagine a world without Evan. Or Ellis, for that matter. God, what the hell had happened to her family?

"Have you heard from Ellis?" Dylan asked as if he'd read her mind.

"I really don't want to talk about my brothers right now." Keeping her mind off them was the only way she was keeping it together. Ellis had only been missing a week and she was hoping he reached out to her soon.

He simply nodded as they reached his office. "I'm still waiting on an answer," he said as they stepped inside.

Yeah, she'd figured that. "I don't know how to give you one— Who's this?" she asked when a chocolate-colored Labrador lifted its head off a giant gray and white dog bed. It eased to its four paws and trotted over to her, sniffing her feet thoroughly before sitting in front of her and waiting for...something.

"Cooper." Dylan's voice softened just a fraction.

Evie reached out slowly and scratched him behind the ears. "I wish I had a treat for you," she murmured.

"He takes belly rubs as well as treats." Dylan's voice was dry. "He uses mind control and guilty looks to get his way. He's completely shameless."

Despite the situation, she let out a startled laugh at his tone. "When did you get him?" she asked as the dog trotted back to his bed and flopped down on it, acting as if walking over to her had been an enormous effort.

"About two weeks after you..." He cleared his throat. "Found him on the side of the road. He'd been hit by a car, had a broken leg. Wasn't microchipped and couldn't find an owner so...I kept him. Vet thinks he's about five years old." His tone completely softened when he talked about Cooper.

"He's adorable." She kept her gaze on Cooper so she wouldn't have to look at Dylan.

"You going to answer my question?" he asked, drawing her gaze up to him.

"Which one?"

His eyes were shards of green glass as he folded his arms over his chest. "Why'd you walk out on me? On us?"

How the hell could she answer him? She couldn't tell him the real reason she'd ended things after he'd proposed. Their entire meeting had been a lie. He'd fallen in love with Evie, the woman who worked for a non-profit, the woman who enjoyed wine tastings and black-tie parties. Not the woman who enjoyed hand-to-hand sparring, hockey games and drinking beer with her crew whenever she had down time. She could play the polished socialite, but it wasn't her. And he deserved the truth, not what she'd fed him. The only thing that hadn't been a lie had been the connection—and the sex. Holy hell, that had been raw, real and something she'd never imagined was possible. "I walked away because it would be easier for both of us. You didn't really love me." It hurt her to say it, but he deserved to hear it.

He let out a harsh laugh. "Is that right? Please tell me more about my thoughts and feelings."

She balled her fingers into fists at her side. "You don't know the real me," she snapped. Hell, she was giving away more than she should.

"Is that right?"

"That is right. Tonight should make that pretty damn obvious."

His gaze narrowed slightly. "I'm going to go out on a limb and say you don't work for a nonprofit?"

She turned away from him, stalked to the huge window overlooking the Olympic-sized pool. In the reflection, she could see him behind her leaning against his desk, his body bowstring tight. She closed her eyes and rubbed the back of her neck as she felt a headache creeping in. "No, I don't."

"So what do you do for a living? I'm assuming it has to do with not being able to call the cops tonight?"

"Sort of, yes. I don't work with Samara anymore. But I used to. We used to be partners of sorts."

"Are you going to tell me what tonight is all about, then?"

Sighing, she turned back around to face him and was struck by the iciness in his eyes. Sure, she deserved it, but that didn't mean she liked it. More than anything she wished things could be different. But she couldn't regret what she'd done because she'd saved a lot of lives. A lot of innocent children and women had been saved from a life of slavery because of the Jensen op. "I honestly don't know what's going on with her right now. But I will find out."

He stared at her for a long moment before motioning to one of the seats by his desk. "Why don't you sit? You look exhausted."

She was, it was true. All the stress and pressure from everything going on with her family was pushing in on her, making it hard to think straight. Now she had to face Dylan again, had to face her past.

Before she could take a step toward the chair, Finn opened the office door. He nodded politely at her then looked at Dylan even as Cooper got up and nudged Finn's hand, urging him to pet his head. "My patient is fine. Now why the hell aren't we calling the cops?" he asked, even as he absently petted the Lab.

"Is she awake?" Evie asked, not waiting for Dylan to answer him.

Finn looked back at her now. "Yes, she's—"

"Is she okay enough to move to another location?" She wanted to get Samara out of here for a couple reasons. One of them was purely selfish—she needed distance from Dylan—but she really wanted to draw any potential danger away from him. He hadn't signed on for anything and Evie wasn't sure what was going on yet.

"You're not going anywhere," Dylan snapped.

She pinned him with a dark look. "If we stay here, you could be in danger. I literally don't know what this was about. I don't think we were followed, but even so,

I'm not taking the chance that you get caught in the crossfire of whatever this is."

"Don't act like you care what happens to me," he snapped out, fire and anger in his words.

"I *do* care!" And that was pure, raw truth. She cared far too much what happened to this man. He had never just been a mark, an asset. Maybe at first, for a hot second, she had thought he would be the perfect asset. But then she'd gotten to know him. He'd gotten into her head, under her skin, and into her bed. And she never slept with assets. Sleeping with him hadn't been part of the job either.

No...Dylan had been different. She'd never expected him. Never expected to want him. He'd completely blown up her entire world. Then she'd had to walk away. And she'd missed him ever since. It was like her mind had been in a state of disarray since Dylan and she couldn't get back on track. Couldn't compartmentalize. It was part of the reason she'd left the Agency. She hadn't been able to do her job anymore. Not the way she'd been able to before.

Something in his expression shifted but she couldn't read what had changed. "Whatever the problem is, she'll be safe here. Leo's got the house and property on lockdown. It was already secure, but since you two showed up he's gone into overkill. And you know he's the best."

She could give him that. Leo Webster was definitely good at his job. Former military, former FBI, the man knew his stuff. So that kinda killed her argument for leaving, damn it. She looked at Finn. "Can I see her?" Mainly because she needed to find out what the hell was going on, and she could admit she needed to get away from Dylan and what he made her feel.

"She's okay to talk. For now. But she needs rest."

That was all Evie needed to hear.

As she made her way through the house, her phone buzzed in her pocket. When she saw her mom's name on the screen, she winced. She should've been back at the hospital hours ago. "Mom, I'm sorry I didn't make it back. Something important came up. I swear I would have been back otherwise."

"It's okay." Her mom sounded exhausted. "Nothing's changed. Your father and I are going to go home and grab a couple hours of sleep. I just called to tell you not to bother coming back tonight."

Even though there wasn't an ounce of censure in her mom's words, she still felt a punch of guilt straight through her heart. "Oh, Mom, I'm coming back."

"Honey, I'm serious. Just get a little sleep. I know this is hard on everyone. Isla is staying. I can't convince her to leave."

Her brother's fiancée. "Have the doctors said anything positive?"

"Well, his vitals are stable and nothing has gotten worse so they're taking that as a good sign."

"Okay. I love you, Mom."

"I love you too."

As she disconnected, she eased open the door to Samara's room and found her friend fast asleep. *Damn it.*

Evie wanted to wake her up but wasn't sure if she should. Her friend had arrived with no electronics, and for that matter, Evie hadn't even seen a vehicle near her brother's house. Damn it, she should have asked her more questions when she'd had the chance.

Sighing, she stepped back out of the room and quietly shut the door behind her—and nearly ran into Leo as she headed back down the hallway.

"Ms. Bishop." Ice dripped from those two words. A tall, handsome man in his early fifties, he had sharp, brown eyes as dark as his skin. He'd been with the bureau for years before putting in his resignation—to finally settle down with his wife—and Dylan had scooped him up.

He wasn't even bothering to hide his disdain for Evie, and even though she didn't blame him, she simply nodded at him, having absolutely no energy right now to deal with anything more.

"What kind of danger have you brought into this house?" he asked when she would have stepped around him.

"I won't be here long."

"That is not what I asked." Each word was clipped.

"Fine, I don't know. So I guess just assume the worst kind of danger."

He nodded once, watching her carefully. "With the women Dylan dated before you, I always ran deep scans on them. But because you're a Bishop, my scan was cursory. I knew you weren't after him for his money. Once you left him, I ran another one. What I found was interesting."

Surprised he'd told her so much, she simply lifted an eyebrow because she was in no mood to spar, verbally or otherwise. "Is that right?"

"What I found, or I should say, what I did *not* find was quite interesting." Again with that pointed look.

"Interesting?"

"Yes, interesting. The record of your personal life is ridiculously clean. So mundane it appears to be professionally created. Now you show up on Dylan's doorstep with a gunshot victim. I find it all very interesting."

"Good for you," she said, stepping around him, not putting any heat into her words.

She actually liked Leo. Back when she'd been dating Dylan, Leo had offered to show her how to shoot—because he'd wanted her to be able to protect herself—and she hadn't had the heart to tell him she was an excellent shot. So she'd allowed him to "teach" her how to use a pistol. It had been painful to fake and not be able to show off her skills.

If there was ever a next time, she was going to show him exactly how good she was. Not that any of that mattered now. The man genuinely cared for Dylan and he was just doing his job. A job he was good at.

It wasn't his fault she used to be a spy.

CHAPTER THREE

D ylan looked up from his laptop when his office door opened. Though trying to work had been a joke at this point, he hadn't been certain how long Evie would be with Samara so he'd at least attempted to get some done. The effort had been fruitless, however, because all he'd been able to do was obsess over her.

Evie stepped inside the room, her jet-black hair pulled back into a ponytail, showing off her sharp cheekbones and the faint circles under her eyes. She immediately shut the door behind her.

He knew she was dealing with a lot—one brother in a coma, the other wanted for murder, and now whatever the hell this was with her friend. He might want to pressure her right now for answers, but if he had learned anything from his time with her, pushing her never got him anywhere. Only patience did. Of course, now he was wondering if everything between them was a lie, so what did he know?

"She's asleep." Her blue eyes flashed with annoyance as she said it.

"Just stay here tonight."

She shook her head, even as Cooper made his way over to her, silently begging for her to rub his head. She scratched Cooper's head, seemingly absently, which he was eating up. "I...shouldn't. And I really am sorry I brought this crap to your doorstep. I just didn't know who else to turn to."

He believed her. Because he couldn't think that she would have turned to him unless she had no other option. That thought didn't sit well with him either. "I've got food if you're hungry and you can take a shower in one of the guest rooms. I've got clothes you can wear as well." He might be angry at her, but he still cared for her. Still...nope. Not going there. He'd thought he could force himself to get over her, and for the last six months he'd thrown himself into work, killing himself with endless days at his desk and in meetings so that he had no down time, no time to think about her. Except it hadn't worked, because he still wasn't over her.

She frowned, crossing her arms over her chest—which just made Cooper sulk and head back to his over-stuffed bed. Her upper arms were muscled, but not bulkily. She had a runner's body, lean and toned, and he knew she got in a lot of practice on her punching bag. "I'm fine, but thank you."

There was something in her tone that made him pause. "What the hell, Evie? Just stay here. Your friend is here, so it's stupid to leave. And I'm sure you haven't had much other than hospital food, so you'll eat too." Damn it, she pissed him off.

She looked surprised, but nodded. "Fine, but I'm not putting on some stranger's clothes."

He blinked at her odd tone. "They're *your* clothes. You left some here when you..."

She paused. "I did?"

He nodded. She'd left a handful of things and he'd never been able to get rid of them. He wasn't sure what that said about him other than he was a masochist. For her.

The tension in her shoulders eased. "Okay, thank you. For everything. You're being very generous." Her words were stilted, however, and they pissed him off.

Because he hated that she was still talking to him like he was a goddamn stranger. But maybe that was all they were. Strangers. No, he refused to believe that. Not when he knew how she sounded when she came, how she looked... How she liked her coffee in the morning. "Come on. You can stay in the room next to your friend's."

She nodded and followed him out—and Cooper wasn't far behind, curious about their new visitor.

He ignored the familiar vanilla scent that teased his nose, the scent that was all Evie. The one that made him think of twisted, tangled sheets and her pinned underneath him.

The one that haunted him when he closed his eyes.

* * *

Evie turned on the shower in Dylan's luxurious guest bathroom. It was weird to be in here instead of in his room. Of course if he'd offered to share his room, she would've been more than surprised. Hell, she was surprised he was insisting that she stay here regardless. He should have kicked her out on her ass. Which just drove home the point of what a decent man he was, and made her feel worse about her previous deception while they'd been together.

Instead of stripping, she quickly called her former coworker, letting the running water block any other outside sounds.

Benjamin Miller—or simply Ben—answered on the third ring, his tone distracted, and she heard the faint click of a keyboard in the background. "Yeah?"

"Hey, it's Evie. Is this a bad time?"

"It's always a bad time, but I'll spare a few minutes for one of my favorite people."

She snorted softly and hopped up on the countertop. "Samara called me earlier with some interesting news." She wasn't going to tell Ben that Samara had actually stopped by after being shot. Some things she would keep to herself until she knew more.

He sighed, as if he wasn't surprised. "I've had half a dozen conversations with her. There is no fucking con-spiracy."

Since Evie wasn't completely certain what was going on—since Samara hadn't told her everything—she had to play this carefully and act as if she already knew. "You know what Samara is like though. She's like a freaking dog with a bone once she gets something in her head."

"Yeah, I know. But Xiao died of a heart attack and Kalinec was killed in a mugging gone wrong—and while I am definitely saddened by their deaths, it was bad luck. Really bad luck. I've done my due diligence and there is no connection between their deaths and the Jensen op. I respect Samara, obviously, but...I don't know what's going on in her head to make this connection."

Evie had worked with Xiao and Kalinec—two skilled operators—on the Jensen op, but while she knew them, they hadn't been friends. Just skilled coworkers. She hadn't even found out about their deaths until Samara had told her, since she'd already left the Agency. Now it seemed Samara thought they'd been killed in some sort of conspiracy? Or at least that was what Ben made it sound like. "So you think she's overreacting?" But Evie didn't think so. If the two men were dead and Samara had been shot, something was going on at least.

"I didn't say that. I just don't think there's some weird conspiracy tying these deaths to the Jensen job like she thinks. We took that fucker down and everyone involved with him. We literally cut off all the links. This isn't some revenge thing—there's no one who could want revenge. I've run the data and it keeps telling me the same thing. She wants to see something that isn't there."

Samara's bullet wound said otherwise. But Evie kept that to herself for right now. "Okay, just wanted to check with you. I know what she's like," she said, laughing even though she didn't mean it. She liked Ben, had done more than a handful of ops with him, but he was definitely an analyst. He was all about the numbers and not gut instinct. And maybe he was right, maybe the deaths had been random, but...Samara had been shot. So Evie was going to get to the bottom of that at least.

"I tried calling her but she hasn't responded," he continued. "I think she's pissed at me."

No, she's passed out in the room next to mine, recovering from a gunshot wound. She kept the thought to herself. "I talked to her a couple times about all this. I'll soothe her feathers next time I hear from her."

"Thanks. How's civilian life, anyway?"

"Eh. Dealing with a lot of family shit right now."

"Right..." He sounded distracted. "Let me know if you need anything."

"Will do." Evie might not be CIA anymore but she still had top-level clearance, at least for another six months. If she did need help, she'd reach out to him.

Once they disconnected, she set her phone on the countertop and stripped off her clothes. The bathroom had already filled with steam, and the moment she stepped under the pulsing jets she allowed herself a fraction of relief.

Her life had imploded but she was going to enjoy this damn shower for the next few minutes. God, even Dylan's shampoo and body wash was the luxury kind—fifty dollars for a teeny bottle. She wondered if Dylan had put this in here especially for her or if this was simply how he stocked his guest bathroom. She cursed herself for caring at all. It didn't matter. No way he'd done anything special for her. He was probably counting down the seconds until he could get rid of her, and she wouldn't blame him if he was.

She had no future with Dylan Blackwood. He was a former lover, a former asset, former...everything.

He sure as hell wasn't part of her future though. Even if she wanted him to be.

Because if she allowed herself to even think that might be possible, she would have to acknowledge that she would have to tell him the truth. And if she did that, he'd leave her for sure. So she was cutting things off as soon as possible.

Unfortunately she had to figure out who the hell had shot Samara and why. Because an unknown enemy wanted Samara dead. And an unknown enemy was the worst kind.

Damn it, so much for a peaceful shower. Her brain simply wouldn't shut off as she started running through potential enemies of Samara's. And the list was long.

* * *

"I lost her," the male voice on the other end said.

He gritted his teeth and forced himself to take a deep breath. "How is that possible?" He needed Samara taken care of. Nosy bitch. Why couldn't she just leave well enough alone?

"She's good. What can I say? The target must have ditched her vehicle, but I know I shot her. She hasn't shown up at any walk-in clinics or ERs in the sur-rounding areas. And there have been no reports of gun-shot victims matching her description. So she's potentially dead, which I doubt. Or she found someone to take the bullet out for her. Or hell, she took it out herself."

He was quiet for a long moment as he digested the words, his mind going into overdrive. "She'll need antibiotics."

Unfortunately the woman was trained and could get shit like that herself. She could simply steal them.

The man on the other end of the line was silent, forcing him to talk again. "I'll double your fee if you find her," he said. Because he needed Samara gone. She was sticking her nose where it didn't belong. And while she didn't have all the facts, she was invested in finding out more and that meant trouble for him.

He enjoyed his life and he would not let her screw things up because of her curiosity. Because sooner or later she was going to get Evie Bishop stirred up. Those two had always had each other's backs.

And if both of them came for him... *No.* He would simply have to take care of Samara and eliminate that possibility. Maybe he would take care of Samara himself. He knew she was somewhere in Miami. And she couldn't hide forever. He would make damn sure of it.

CHAPTER FOUR

Though it was nearly four in the morning, Evie was now awake so she searched out Samara. She'd always been like that: once she woke up—because her brain wouldn't let her rest—she was up for good.

As she entered the room, she was surprised to find Finn sitting by Samara's bedside, her friend propped up and looking paler than last night. But at least she was awake. And Cooper was lounging on the bed next to her, looking as if he owned the place.

"Hey," she said, keeping her voice low, leaving the door open. "How are you feeling?"

"Good enough. Apparently I have an infection." She shifted slightly, then tried to cover up a wince. "But at least I've got this adorable mutt to keep me company."

As if he knew he was being talked about, Cooper lifted his head and licked Samara's hand.

"You did the right thing by bringing her here," Finn continued, closing his little doctor's bag. "Of course a hospital would've been better." His tone was dry but not too judgmental. She'd only met Finn a couple times and he'd always seemed like a decent guy. Her opinion of him had only gone up now.

"I need a few minutes alone with Samara." And she wasn't asking.

The doctor nodded and stood. "I'll be in the kitchen getting coffee if you need me. Come on, Coop."

The dog groaned but jumped off the bed, following after the doctor.

She waited until Finn was gone, then peered out the door just to make sure he wasn't eavesdropping. Not that she really expected him to.

"How are you feeling, really?" she asked, sitting next to her friend.

"I've felt worse." Samara lifted a shoulder. "I've also felt better." Her smile was wry.

"I'm glad you're okay." She cleared her throat. "So I called Ben."

She pursed her lips together. "I figured you would. What did he say?"

"Enough that I figured out what's going on with you. He said he's investigated everything and run all analyses on the two deaths."

"I know. But my gut tells me something different. Maybe the deaths aren't connected to the Jensen job but it feels too weird that Xiao and Kalinec died so close together."

"Maybe..." But shit happened. Evie knew that more than most. Look at her family right now. "So how did you get shot? I want all the details."

"Seamus is in Miami and I'd planned to see him as well as you."

Seamus was in Miami? He'd been on the op along with Xiao, Kalinec and Luca Ramos, though Seamus had been on the periphery, lending support with Ben.

"Yeah. And between us, I'm not even supposed to know that, but I had one of the guys run some facial recognition software for me. Under the radar. Not sure what Seamus is doing here though. I couldn't get a hit on his phone or bank accounts...nothing."

Evie frowned at that, thinking of the handsome Seamus who she'd run half a dozen ops with. He'd asked her out more than once—and she'd always said no. He was a good agent and a decent enough guy, but she'd never dated in the workplace. Far too messy. "I thought he found work in the private sector."

"I did too. I just wanted to talk to him, see if he remembered anything from the op that I'm not seeing. Then this happened so I decided to come straight to you."

"We'll see what we can figure out. I've got to grab my laptop from my brother's house. But I've got pretty much every ounce of information on the Jensen files memorized regardless." Evie had lived and breathed that job until the very end.

"Yeah, me too. None of this makes sense. There is literally no obvious person gunning for us."

She was right. Rod Jensen had been a real estate mogul in Miami who'd been busy trafficking people, among other things. A real sick bastard. And their team had helped expose him. Luckily there was a loophole for the CIA when it came to investigations—they were able to investigate anywhere, but the FBI had to handle the arrests on US soil. So they'd tag-teamed with the Feds, and Jensen had been taken down. A win-win for everyone. And Jensen hadn't had any angry partners or relatives or anyone who would want revenge against Evie's team. Not to mention, their involvement had been very quiet. The Feds had gotten all the credit for his takedown while her team had been in the background.

"Exactly, which makes me think this has to do with something completely different. You've got a lot of enemies. We need to broaden our suspect pool to see who wants you dead."

"I hate it when you're right... So what's up with you and Blackwood?" Samara gave her a sly grin.

"Nothing. He's letting you stay here. Not really sure why." She didn't want to think too hard on the reason either.

Samara shifted against the pillow. "Really? You're not sure?"

"Shut up. You should be focusing on figuring out who shot you, dumbass."

"I always have time for gossip. And I've already compiled a mental list of who might want me dead. I just need to pull files."

Evie nodded and stood. "I'll help. Where's your stash house?" Because Samara had to have stashed her stuff somewhere in Miami. She'd shown up on Evie's doorstep with nothing but the clothes on her back and a bullet in her hip.

Samara only paused for a moment before rattling off the name of a self-storage company.

"All right. I'll grab your stuff and my laptop. Have you talked to Luca about any of this?"

"No, he's out of the country. Didn't want to bother him."

"Okay. I'll be back... You need anything right now?"

Samara shook her head, her eyes starting to drift. "Nah. Gonna get a little sleep though," she murmured.

"Good." She glanced at her phone, her heart rate kicking up when she saw the message from her mom. "I'll be a little longer," she told her friend.

But by then Samara had already dozed off.

* * *

Dylan stood waiting outside the guest room, unabashedly eavesdropping on Evie and her friend. He hadn't heard everything, but he'd heard enough. As she stepped out of the room, she paused once in clear surprise to see him, but just as quickly her face went into that neutral mask that he hated. It pissed him off when she shut him out. When they'd been together, she'd been so smooth about it and it had grated on his nerves.

"Did you mean it when you said my friend could stay here?" she asked, apparently ignoring his eavesdropping.

"Yes. I mean what I say." The dig was unnecessary and he felt like a dick the second after the words were out because of the flicker of hurt in her eyes, but he couldn't take it back. He could stop being an asshole at least. Because he didn't like being this guy.

"Good. I need to go to the hospital. My mom texted me. Evan is awake."

Oh, hell. "I'll drive."

"Dylan, you don't need to go with me. It's four in the morning and you've got an entire empire to run." There was only a hint of dryness as she said the word empire.

"Don't bother arguing." He was friends with both her brothers, regardless of what had happened between him and Evie. And he was also friends with her parents. Though he'd kept his distance from all of them in the last six months. Ever since Evie had walked out on him with a half-assed excuse about not being ready for marriage.

She looked as if she wanted to push back, but she simply said, "Okay. Can we stop and grab something on the way? I'm sure Isla hasn't eaten anything in ages and I want to bring her breakfast."

"We don't need to stop. There's plenty here we can pack up." The woman who cooked for him often left plenty of baked goods and other things he never touched. But his security guys loved it so he left it all out for them.

It only took a few minutes to gather everything before they were on the road.

Evie was dressed in a pair of jeans and a long-sleeved black sweater, both items she'd left at his house months ago. Her inky black hair was down around her shoulders, wavy and loose, and she didn't have on makeup again. She looked younger than her twenty-eight years like that, though stress lines bracketed her eyes and mouth. No wonder, considering what she was dealing with. She was still lean and fit, as she'd been months ago. Nothing had changed.

Except...everything had.

"Is there any news on the bombing of Evan's office?" The one that had killed half a dozen people and injured a lot more, including Evan himself, only three weeks ago.

"Not that I know of. I know the FBI agent in charge, however. I've talked to her a couple times and she says they're making progress. I believe her too." Evie's words were matter-of-fact.

And very telling. "You know the FBI agent personally?"

She paused and rubbed her fingers against her temple. "Yeah," she muttered. "I do."

"Did you use to be a Fed?" Because she'd been in some type of law enforcement, he just wasn't certain which branch. He'd told Leo to hold off running any more security checks on her. He wanted her to tell him herself. He didn't want more lies between them.

"No."

"Then who did you work for? DEA? DIA? CIA?" He was simply shooting in the dark here.

"It's a three-letter acronym. And it's all I'm going to tell you right now."

Right now? He'd take it. "Is that why you ended things with me? Because of your job?" It would make more sense than what she'd told him.

Instead of answering, she looked out the window, her jaw tight.

Dylan wanted to shake the answers out of her but knew that wasn't possible. Tension spread across his shoulders, all his muscles tightening. "The way you ended things with me was shitty."

"I know." She wouldn't look at him.

He wanted to push but they were on the way to the hospital to see her brother and family. And what else was there to say now? He'd asked her to marry him, she'd said no, telling him she didn't want to live in Miami or get married. Then she'd cut off contact and moved back to DC—only to come back to Miami not long afterward. And he hadn't seen her in the months since then.

"So what's up with your friend?" he asked. "And what can I do to help?"

She turned to look at him as they pulled up to a stoplight, her expression a mix of emotions. Confusion was one of them. "You're already helping by giving her a safe haven. And why the hell *are* you helping me?"

"Because you need it." Yes, she'd hurt him, but that didn't erase the fact that he still cared for her—more than just cared. And no matter how hard he might try, he wasn't cold enough to turn his back on Evie Bishop when she needed help.

She let out a strangled sound and turned away from him again. "You make me insane."

"Me helping you makes you insane?" He snorted.

"This would be a lot easier if you were a giant dick."

"I can work on that, then. I'll be meaner if you'd prefer." He'd thought he was doing a pretty good job of being a jerk.

She snorted out laughter at his words, and despite the tension and unspoken things between them, he smiled as well.

God, he'd missed her.

* * *

Evie resisted the strange urge to link her fingers through Dylan's as they stepped out of the elevator. They weren't a couple, and really, they never had been. Everything had been fake.

As they headed down the tiled hallway, she prepared herself for the worst and hoped for the best.

To her surprise, Dylan squeezed her shoulder once before letting his arm drop. "I'm staying here with you," he said as they entered into the small private waiting room. Her parents had donated a ton of money to this hospital, so yeah, they'd sectioned off a waiting room for her family.

Her mom's gaze flicked to Dylan's once in surprise as the two of them entered together, but she immediately pulled Evie into a tight hug. "Evan's awake but he won't see any of us," she said as she stepped back. She'd given up on makeup days ago. Her eyes were puffy from crying and she looked as if she'd aged a decade.

Evie certainly felt as if she had. "That can't be right."

She looked over at Isla—the sophisticated redhead who was always so put-together—and her brother's fiancée looked as if she hadn't slept in a week. Evie feared she probably hadn't. Her normally beautifully curled auburn tresses were pulled back into a sharp ponytail, and dark circles ringed underneath her eyes. "It's true. He won't even see me." Isla said the words as if she couldn't comprehend them at all.

Evie didn't either. "I want to see the doctor," she snapped out.

"Your father is with him now," her mom said, shaking her head. "It won't do any good."

Evie turned to look at Dylan, grateful and confused that he was here at all. "I'll be back," she murmured as he set out the bag of food he'd brought. She heard him offering to grab drinks for both women as she stepped out of the room and ran right into her father.

"What's going on?" she demanded.

"Your brother won't see any of us." Her father, tall and strong, with salt and pepper hair, looked ready to fall over.

"Where is he?"

He gently grasped her shoulders as he looked down at her. "I know you want to storm in there, but it won't do any good. He doesn't give permission for any of us to come see him. We can't ignore his wishes."

"I don't understand."

Her father rubbed a hand over his face and for the first time ever looked almost breakable. Sighing, he said, "The doctor said he isn't handling things well. He's completely cognizant and understands what happened. But his face is burned and he's definitely going to have scarring. He...he doesn't want to see any of us. Not even Isla."

"When he's better I'm going to kick his ass for this," she growled even though she knew this had nothing to do with them, but her brother's own fears. She just hated that they couldn't be there for him.

Her father seemed startled by her declaration and pulled her into a tight hug. "I'm so glad you're back in Miami," he murmured, his voice thick with unshed tears.

She hugged him tightly. "I am too. He'll change his mind." Evan had to. Dashing away the wetness on her cheeks, she stepped back.

"I certainly hope so."

Dylan stepped out of the room then and she saw the same look of surprise flicker across her father's features. He held out a hand to Dylan and shook it once.

"William," Dylan said quietly, taking his hand. "I'm going to grab some coffee for Eleanor and Isla. Do you guys want anything?" he asked, all civil politeness.

Her father started to shake his head but then said, "Yes. I'll come with you."

Feeling at a loss in general, Evie stepped back into the room, letting them go off together. Her father and Dylan had always gotten along.

She picked up a blueberry muffin and set it in front of Isla. "I know you're not hungry, but you've got to eat something. You look like hell."

To her surprise, Isla didn't argue with her, simply tore off part of the top and shoved it in her mouth. Gone was the graceful woman she knew. She sat there chewing for what seemed like forever, finally swallowing some of it down. Then she dropped the rest of the muffin onto the table. "I don't understand why he doesn't want to see me." She broke on the last word, her tears a river on her cheeks.

Evie wrapped her arms around Isla, holding her tight. "He's gone through a trauma. He's not thinking about anything other than himself right now, which is totally normal and fair." She hoped that sounded good because she was just pulling words out of her ass. Isla had lost a hell of a lot in that bombing, including her own father. And she'd been sitting here in the waiting room, waiting for the man she loved to wake up for the last three weeks. And now Evan wouldn't see her? God, what a world this was right now. "I'm so sorry, Isla."

"It's not your fault." Isla pulled back and reached for her muffin again, though she didn't make an attempt to eat anything.

As Evie leaned back, her mom swooped in and pulled her into another hug. "You'd better not be leaving Miami anytime soon. I can't lose my kids."

"I swear I'm not going anywhere." If she'd questioned her decision to move home a month ago, she certainly didn't now.

She needed to keep her shit together now above all times. Her parents refused to talk about Ellis at all, even though none of them thought he was guilty. She knew

for a fact he wasn't. Her brother was a freaking Boy
Scout. Unlike her, who liked to work in shades of gray,
Ellis didn't. He was by the book all the way.

She stowed that thought for now and grabbed another muffin for Isla, who'd finally finished the first
one. "Eat. You'll thank me later."

"You're just as bossy as your brother," Isla murmured.

"It's a Bishop quality. We're all bossy and demanding."

Her mom let out a watery laugh. "True enough. So
why is Dylan Blackwood with you?"

"You can't seriously be asking me this right now."
She grabbed a bagel from the stack of food for herself.

"Of course I'm asking you. We're going to be stuck
here for who knows how long and I need something to
take my mind off...everything."

"Honestly, nothing. I just stopped by to see Dylan
about something and then I got your text about Evan."

"You must think I was born yesterday if you think
I'll believe that you stopped by his house at four in the
morning. Because that's when I texted you." Her mom
watched her with the same clear blue eyes that were a
mirror of Evie's own.

She broke her mom's gaze. "That's my story and I'm
sticking to it."

"You're ridiculous," Isla murmured, a smile tugging
at her lips. Then her gaze fell on Evie's shoes. "Almost
as ridiculous as those shoes."

Shrugging, she took a bite of her bagel. Even though she wanted to help her mom and Isla get their minds off Evan, she wasn't going to talk about Dylan.

It was too painful.

CHAPTER FIVE

"You didn't have to stay the whole time," Evie said as Dylan pulled out of the hospital parking garage. The truth was he hadn't needed to come at all, let alone stay until nearly lunch time with her and her family. She wanted to stay longer, but at the same time, there was nothing she could do for Evan or even Isla. And she needed to find out who had shot at Samara. Her parents or Isla would let her know if anything changed with her brother.

"I wanted to. So what are you going to do about your friend?"

"Get to the bottom of things." At this point she wasn't sure how much she was going to tell him, even if he was being helpful. The more he knew, the more danger he could be in. "I need to get my laptop from my brother's house." She also needed a few other things, including some burner phones just in case. She'd take some from her stash at the same time she picked up Samara's stash. That would be later—and she'd do it alone. The less time Dylan spent with her in public, the better for him.

He was silent for a long moment then surprised her when he said, "When are you going to start looking for your own place?"

"Ah…soon." Of course, she hadn't really looked because she'd been taking her time figuring out her next move. She'd already gotten a few job offers for security consulting, but…she wasn't ready to pull the trigger on anything yet. "I could always move in with my parents," she said dryly.

He snorted softly at that. Her parents were wonderful but they could definitely be a bit much, and she liked her space and her privacy.

"So what's going on with Ellis?" he asked.

She was surprised he was asking about her other brother again.

Even though she didn't want to talk about her family, she figured Dylan deserved pretty much any truth she could give him at this point, considering the secrets she was keeping from him. "I'm not sure. I mean, like I told you before, I know he's innocent. And I've tried digging into what happened, but I got stonewalled by the damn Feds. Mostly. The agent in charge gave me some information. Just not enough." She left out the part that she'd asked a friend to hack into some files for her. "I have no doubt that he was set up." She'd gotten that much from the files alone. Her brother was too damn smart to get caught killing someone, so he'd definitely been set up. Not that the Boy Scout would have killed someone in cold blood anyway.

"Is there anything I can do to help?"

She glanced at him in surprise. "Are you sure you haven't had enough of my drama?"

"I'm pretty sure I'll never get enough of your drama."
His eyes sparked with heat as he spoke.

Oh, hell. She wasn't sure how to take that so she
turned away, glancing in the side view mirror again. A
four-door gray sedan changed lanes and zipped in front
of another car before shifting in behind the vehicle behind them.

"We've got a tail," Dylan said before she could say
the same, his tone clipped.

"Yeah, three cars back. Gray Nissan."

"That's the one."

It was a neutral, boring car that wouldn't stand out
anywhere. But she was trained to see stuff like that.
And so was he. He'd been in the Marines and in war
zones. He knew when someone was following him.
"They could just be heading in the same direction as
us." Of course if they were, they'd been behind them
since they'd pulled out of the hospital parking lot.

"They could." Dylan took a sharp left turn onto a
residential street.

A few seconds later, the gray car followed, revving
its engine as it sped after them, giving up any pretense
of not following them.

Her heart rate increased as she turned around. This
could be whoever had shot Samara. And if they thought
they could hurt her—or Dylan—she was about to show
them the error of their ways. "Are you armed?" Evie
asked even as a shot of adrenaline punched through
her.

Jaw tense, a short nod.

Why was she not surprised? "Where?"

"One in the center console and one under my seat."

She paused. "Two weapons?"

"I take my security seriously." His gaze flicked to the rearview mirror again.

All right, then. She'd never seen him in action, not in real life anyway. But she'd seen an old satellite video of the man taking enemy fire and holding his own—and saving four men's lives. He could more than take care of himself. She opened his center console. Sure enough, a pistol was tucked inside. Normally she was armed but her weapon was back at his place. Without asking for permission, she plucked his pistol out of its holster.

He frowned at her but didn't tell her to stop. "I'm not getting in a high-speed chase with this guy."

Evie didn't like the idea of that either. Not surrounded by all these residential streets. Too big of a chance of a civilian getting hurt. "You could drive straight to the police station." She hated the idea of losing this guy, but she also wasn't going to let any civilians get hurt. Hell no.

"I have a better idea." He revved the engine, speeding up as he took another sharp turn onto another residential street. Cars lined both sides of the street, some parked in driveways, some on the road.

"What are you doing?" She clutched the grab handle as he tore into an empty driveway and quickly reversed. "Oh shit!"

He gunned the engine, arrowing straight at the gray car.

"Dylan!"

"He'll swerve." The man looked absolutely convinced as he pressed on the gas.

Yeah, well, she wasn't so sure. She pressed the sunroof button, opening it as he sped down the asphalt.

The other car zoomed right at them. Her heart jumped in her chest. The guy wasn't swerving. Neither was Dylan. *Fuuuuccck.*

They were only a few car lengths apart now. *Oh, God.* Her throat seized— The gray car swerved at the last minute.

Heart still pounding, she unstrapped and jumped up, pistol out, and aimed at the rear window. Glass shattered everywhere. She took another shot, this time at one of the tires.

Ping.

Adrenaline pumping, she ducked as a bullet glanced off the top of Dylan's car. Hell, the guy was firing back.

"Evie, get down!"

The Nissan's engine revved, so she took another shot. This time her aim was true.

One of the tires blew but the driver kept going, speeding away.

"Hold tight."

Wind whipped her hair everywhere as he did a sharp U-Turn, chasing after the guy.

"I'm taking that guy down." Or she was assuming it was a guy. Whoever was inside had been wearing a hat and sunglasses, but the build had looked male.

"Shit, Evie, we need to call the cops." Even so, he hadn't slowed down one iota. Cursing, whether in general or at her, she wasn't sure, he increased his speed, taking a sharp right turn after the shooter.

"Ah, hell," she muttered as the Nissan pulled into a parking lot for a local park full of families and children.

The male driver jumped out of the front seat and sprinted across the gravel parking lot toward a field of grass, not looking back to see if he was followed. The guy hurried down a little bridge, his hands in his pockets, moving far too quickly.

Evie cursed again as Dylan put his own car in park. She couldn't follow after the guy into a crowd of innocent people, but she could at least search the car. She motioned to let Dylan know what she was doing as he started talking to the police.

Using the edge of her sweater, she opened the passenger side door and did a quick sweep, but was careful not to touch anything with her bare hands. No surprise, the thing was empty. It wasn't like she'd expected him to leave a driver's license or other incriminating evidence, but a girl could dream.

As she slid back into Dylan's car, he set his phone down. "My detective friend is on the way. He said he's sending some black-and-whites ahead so they can canvas the park."

She rubbed a hand over her face. "I have a concealed weapons permit and a pretty high security clearance," she told him, giving away even more of herself. At this

point... *Hell.* "I don't want any of this on the record.
You think your detective friend can make that happen?"

He eyed her for a long moment, then nodded. "I'll
see what he can do. Do you just want to leave now and
I'll say I shot at the guy?"

"No way. I'll take responsibility for what I did. And
we didn't do anything wrong."

Looking too sexy for his own good, he simply lifted
a shoulder and glanced out at the parking lot.

She did the same, scanning in case their shooter
came back. Though her instinct told her that whoever
he was, he was long gone. Still, she wasn't going to let
her guard down.

Not now, not ever. And she definitely wasn't going
to think about how Dylan had offered to shoulder the
burden of saying he shot at that guy.

Nope.

She regretted that she'd put him in danger at all, that
she'd dragged him into this. He might be trained, but he
hadn't signed up for this. Hadn't signed up for her.

And she didn't deserve him. Even if she desperately
wanted him.

* * *

"What the hell? I didn't authorize you to do that," he
snapped over the line, looking out at the four-story
building across the street.

"What the hell else was I supposed to do?"

"How about not shoot at Evie Bishop?" As far as he knew Bishop wasn't a threat to him. He'd hired someone to take care of Samara because she was nosy, but Bishop was a different matter entirely. She had a powerful family that could potentially come after him if her death was suspicious.

"She knew I was tailing her, and the guy she was with played chicken with me. She shot at me first."

Oh, this was not good. It was salvageable, but...he didn't like it. "Don't do anything until you hear from me." He ended the call, irritated.

He rubbed his fingers against his temple. He hadn't wanted to involve Bishop in this but considering his hired gun had just shot at her, that might complicate things. He could take care of her himself but...he didn't want to get his hands any dirtier than he already had.

He'd created a nice nest egg for himself and he wasn't going to let anyone take that away from him. Ever.

He had to take care of Samara for certain. But if he did that, he would have to take out Bishop too. And that brought its own set of complications.

Not that it mattered now. He would do what had to be done.

CHAPTER SIX

Dylan sat next to Evie on his couch, resisting the urge to reach out and take her hand in his. He didn't have the right to touch her. No matter how much he wanted to.

Detective Carlito Duarte sat across from them, his expression neutral enough. He had high cheekbones, gray eyes, bronzed skin and a charming smile. The man could have been a model, and Dylan found that it bothered him. He'd never been an insecure man, not when it came to sex or women, but he found himself irrationally annoyed that the happily married guy was so damn good-looking as he sat here with Evie.

Dylan had socialized with the detective a few times, usually at informal gatherings, because of his relationship with the owners of Red Stone Security. And while he didn't employ Red Stone directly, he occasionally used them for certain situations. His casual acquaintance with Duarte was enough that the detective hadn't balked when Dylan had called and told him that he and Evie would be leaving the park.

After the officers had shown up, far too many onlookers from the park area had approached, and of course, they'd pulled out their phones. The last thing Evie needed right now was her face splashed around. So he'd decided to leave. Now they sat in one of Dylan's sitting rooms, politely discussing what had happened.

"I wish I had better news," the detective said. "But the car was reported stolen less than three hours ago. And it's been wiped down as far as we can tell. We might get lucky and snag some prints, but in a situation like this it's doubtful. Are you certain you haven't had any threats lately?" he asked, looking between the two of them.

The assumption was that he'd been the target. He had been driving in his own car. But...Dylan was ninety-nine percent certain this was all about Evie and whatever mess she'd gotten into. He wasn't giving any of that away, however.

He leaned back against his couch, keeping his body language casual even though he wanted to throttle whoever had shot at Evie. He wanted to make that guy pay in blood. "Leo handles all of my security. As far as I know there are no current threats against me." He was dealing with a few civil suits. Bogus ones. But that was simply the price of doing business on the scale that he did. He was honest and didn't rip anybody off but that didn't stop the leeches from coming out of the wood-work, trying to score what they perceived as easy money.

"What about you, Ms. Bishop? I've got a call into the agent handling the case of your brother." He cleared his throat, as if he didn't want to bring up her brother.

"The FBI thinks Evan was targeted because of his business dealings—it wasn't something against my family." Her jaw tightened as she spoke.

Duarte simply nodded. "That's what they told me too. But I actually meant Ellis."

Ah, the one wanted for murder.

"Oh..." She looked at Dylan and shrugged. "I don't know why someone would target me because of Ellis. He's in hiding as far as I know. He's never reached out to any of us so I can't help you on that front."

Duarte watched her carefully. "I'm still going to follow up on that thread regardless."

"Thank you, detective." Evie's tone was polite but neutral.

The detective stood and nodded at both him and Evie. "If either of you think of anything, let me know. I'm going to be digging into this, see if I can grab any images from nearby CCTVs, but without a clear description of the shooter... I just want you to keep your expectations realistic. I will suggest that you increase your security around here and in general. Both of you."

"We will," Dylan said, shaking Duarte's hand.

Once the detective was gone, Evie rubbed a hand over her face. "I don't like that you told him you shot that guy's car."

They'd already been over this. "It simply makes things easier. There were no witnesses. It was my gun, registered under my name. And the assumption is very clearly that I was the target. This keeps any focus off you, which I'm sure you want right now. Your family has been through enough." Obviously. Dylan had already let his security team at the house know what had happened, and while Leo wasn't happy, he was doing what he did best. Keeping this estate locked down tight.

"You're right. Thank you again," she murmured, her expression softening.

He gritted his teeth. He didn't want her thanks but he ignored it. "What's our move now?" Leo was trying to figure out who had shot at them but his head of security was basically working blind. Evie had a whole lot of information Dylan needed, and once she gave it to him, maybe then he could help her figure out who was after Samara, and now apparently her. Because right now he felt as if he was groping around in the dark. He didn't even know who she had really worked for. Though he had a guess.

"Like I told you before, I need to grab my laptop. And...I need to grab a stash of some other things. Both mine and Samara's," she told him.

"You're not leaving here." Over his dead body. After what had just happened, he was keeping her under lockdown. He'd also added one of his security guys at the hospital to keep an eye on her family, just in case. Though after the bombing at Bishop Enterprises, the Feds already had a couple guys unobtrusively down there anyway. They were taking what had happened very seriously.

She gritted her teeth. "I have to get my stuff."

"I can give you whatever you need." Hell, why did that sound like it meant something else?

She simply sat there, watching him and not answering.

He sighed. "Fine. Can I send one of my guys to get your things?" Because he wouldn't bend on her staying put where she was safe.

She paused, thinking it over, before she finally nodded. Her clear blue eyes were sharp as she said, "Yes. That's fine. As long as you trust them."

"I do."

CHAPTER SEVEN

One year ago

*D*ylan shot another look at Evie Bishop, even though he should have been listening to whatever it was his mother was saying. He couldn't believe he'd almost ditched this cocktail party. He had a mountain of work to get to, but now...he didn't care. Not as he stared at the toned, sleek woman a few feet away. Her inky black hair was in some sort of fishtail braid, draped over her bare shoulder— and her strapless blue dress the same color as her eyes wrapped around her perfectly. She was lean, as if she was a runner, and though she couldn't be more than five feet five, she somehow seemed taller. Maybe because of her confidence. This woman was...wow.*

"Dear, are you even listening to me?"

Normally he could carry on a couple conversations at the same time. His ability to multitask was part of the reason he was so good at what he did. But right now the only thing he could focus on was Evie Bishop.

The last time he'd seen her she'd been a skinny little kid. Well, not a kid, but a teenager. She'd been sulky and very clearly hadn't wanted to be at the party with her parents. But she'd grown into a beautiful, funny woman. This party wasn't so pointless anymore. He forced his gaze back to his mom. "I'm sorry, what?"

His mother gave him an exasperated look as she patted his arm. "It's okay. I know you're busy. I just wanted to know if you would be attending the Bishops' party next weekend?"

83

"Yes." His mother looked faintly surprised, but then her lips curved upward. No wonder, since he only attended events when they mattered to his business. Small talk and other bullshit weren't his idea of fun. But he would make an exception. Especially now that he had met Evie Bishop. "Will you excuse me for a minute?" he asked even as he pulled out his buzzing phone from his pocket. When he saw the name on the screen, he paused. But in the end, he answered. "Isabel."

"Have I caught you at a bad time?"

"No. But I'm sorry, things aren't working out between us." He winced at his abruptness. He hadn't meant to just blurt it out, but meeting Evie had him off his game.

She paused for a long moment. "You just get right to the point, don't you? I thought we had been having a lovely time together."

Feeling like an ass, he looked out the French doors. Isabel was a wonderful woman. And they had been having a lot of fun in the last month. But things had changed tonight. Evie had changed everything. "We did, and I apologize. I won't be able to see you socially anymore. Thank you for the last month."

She let out a soft sigh. "I can't say I'm not disappointed, but thank you for not texting."

He snorted at that. He wasn't that much of an asshole. It took another minute to get off the phone with her, and once he had, he shoved out a sigh of relief. He and Isabel had been on a few dates over the last month, and while it had been fun, it had been casual to both of them. They hadn't agreed to be exclusive—he hadn't been exclusive with anyone in a long time. Exclusivity demanded time and effort he wasn't willing to put in. Not while he ran his businesses.

But something told him that if he was going to pursue Evie, she would demand exclusivity. And even if she didn't, he would. He wasn't sure what the hell was going on with *him but he found himself more attracted to her than he'd ever been attracted to anyone. It was like he'd been struck with that proverbial bolt of lightning. It was...disconcerting.*

But he was going to start whatever this thing was between them on the right foot. Hell, he was getting ahead of himself, considering he hadn't even asked her out on a date. He'd sensed that electrical current between them, however.

And he always got what he wanted. He just hoped this time would be no different. Because he wanted Evie Bishop— in his bed and in his life. He'd seen that spark of hunger in her eyes when they'd first met, when they'd shaken hands. It was impossible to deny a connection like that.

CHAPTER EIGHT

"Oh Seamus, you fucker." Evie glared at her computer screen. Ever since Dylan's guy had returned with her and Samara's things, she and Samara had been holed up, digging for information on their laptops well into the afternoon.

"What have you got?" Samara asked, leaning back against the pillow in the bed. She'd told Evie that she was feeling better but Evie wasn't so sure.

"Reached out to a friend of mine who did some deep digging. Turns out that Seamus left the Agency in disgrace months ago. A bunch of money from a black ops slush fund went missing."

Samara let out a low whistle, her eyes widening. "Are you serious? I haven't heard a thing about that."

"Well, the money was for black ops anyway so it technically didn't exist...but it's gone and now he's in Miami. I still can't imagine why he'd want to kill us but he's here, and he's a link to the Jensen op." And now Evie wanted to talk to him.

"Man, I thought he was here for a new job." Samara popped a Cheeto in her mouth as she pushed her own laptop to the side. "How'd you find him?"

Evie shifted on the bed and showed Samara her laptop. "Look at this."

Samara glanced at the screen. "The image is grainy, but...it looks like him. How did you get this?"

"I tapped an asset for a favor. They ran a cursory scan and came up with this. But it was all they could get. So I pulled up some old info on him that I have and it turns out he might be using an alias that he used on an op with me. Which isn't very creative, but..." She shrugged.

"I'm going to nail his ass to the wall," Samara growled.

"I'm going to see what else I can find. You can't leave the house but I can, so—"

"You're not going anywhere alone."

"Well you certainly aren't coming with me. You've been shot. *Shot*."

"Yeah and I'm fine." Samara stood from the bed, wincing, but she did her own version of a model's cat-walk as she strolled up and down the length of the room—limping and hiding her groans of pain.

"Will you please sit down? You look ridiculous." Evie turned back to her laptop as she continued. "If for some reason he's the one who tried to kill you, you can't be showing your face around Miami."

"News flash, you were shot at too." Samara groaned as she got back into bed.

"True enough." It hadn't been the first time, and even though she hoped it would be the last, she wasn't betting on it. "But *I'm* not injured. And I'll go out wearing a disguise." That was part of the reason she'd needed her stash bag. Supplies.

Samara fell back against her pillow. "Fine. But I really am good enough to move around right now. Hey, is the doctor single?"

Evie got whiplash at the change in topic, but she'd learned long ago that was how Samara's brain worked. She often just blurted out whatever she was thinking. "Finn?"

"Yeah. I'd like to take a bite out of him."

"I don't know, want me to pass a note in gym class and ask him?" She rolled her eyes.

Samara simply grinned. "I need a way to pass the time since you won't let me have any fun. And he said he was going to be checking up on me this afternoon."

"The only way you're going to pass the time is with rest and sleep."

Samara simply shrugged, a wicked glint in her eyes.

Evie ignored that look and got back on track. "I'm going to bring Dylan in on some of this." Even if she didn't like the thought of it, she needed someone she could trust to have her back if she approached Seamus. But it grated on her that she might be putting him in danger. And she knew that if she tried to keep him out of anything, he'd just barrel in and help no matter what.

"I know you're not asking me for permission." Samara popped another Cheeto in her mouth.

"No. But I still want your opinion." Evie had run her options over in her head and they were limited right now. She was pretty certain she was being watched, at least by the DEA since Ellis had been a DEA agent and

she was staying at his house. She wasn't under deep surveillance, but she had a feeling she was on their periphery because of her missing brother. They sure as shit
weren't tapping her phone though, that much she'd
made sure of.

That wasn't even her main concern now. No...Dylan
was. Damn it, everything was so complicated with him
involved. Thankfully Dylan was smart and took his security seriously. Not to mention he had resources. So
while she might not want to be linked to him—only for
her own sanity and his safety—right now she needed
the help and she wasn't afraid to ask for it.

"I think it's a great idea. He's not a dumbass so you
won't have to hold his hand for stuff. And he's got a ton
of resources he'd probably let you tap." She grinned
widely. "He'd also probably let you tap that ass if—"

"Oh my God, stop. What the hell is wrong with
you?"

"I'm horny, that's what. I don't like being cooped
up."

"It's only been a day."

"One day too long." Her well-trained friend crossed
her arms over her chest, actually sulking.

Sighing, Evie stood. "Masturbate or something,
then. Just get over whatever this is—and don't proposi-
tion Dylan's doctor. He's doing us a big favor by not
calling the cops."

"No promises."

Ignoring her, she said, "I'm going to find Dylan."
Hopefully he'd be up for a little recon. Or he would just

toss her out of his office and tell her to deal with her own stuff. Evie would find out soon enough. Though deep down, she knew what he was going to say. Because Dylan was a good guy. One who deserved an actual society princess, not...her.

When she opened the door she found Cooper, as if he'd been waiting to be let inside. After nudging Evie for a head rub, he bounded into the room and jumped up next to Samara, cuddling against her. Samara grumbled about him trying to steal her Cheetos but started scratching him behind the ears.

A few minutes later, Evie found Dylan in his office with Leo.

Leo's look wasn't as frosty today but he wasn't friendly either. He simply nodded politely at her as he left, his gaze as shrewd as ever. She wondered how deep he'd dug into her. Not that it mattered—he wouldn't have been able to get much. Nothing other than what she wanted the world to see.

She shut the door behind Leo and turned to Dylan who was sitting behind his desk, his computer in front of him.

"Are you busy? Never mind, of course you are. Dumb question." Why did she have to turn into a rambling moron around him?

He pushed up from his seat and rounded the desk, leaning against it. "What's up? Samara all right?"

"She's good. Whiny, but good." She rolled her eyes. "So...how involved do you want to be with all this stuff

I'm dealing with?" Ugh, she hated that she needed to ask him.

He watched her carefully. "Lay out whatever you've got for me."

She shoved her hands in her jeans pockets. "I can't tell you who I used to work for but you pretty much guessed one of the right acronyms earlier." His jaw twitched so she continued. "I told you two people from an op Samara and I worked on have died fairly close together. Another guy from that op—Seamus—was fired from his job in disgrace and is now in Miami. It looks as if he took a bunch of money too. I have no clue if he's involved in shooting Samara and then shooting at me. But...he's nearby and I want to talk to him."

"How do you know he's here?"

"I have an image of him leaving a local bank. It's kinda grainy but I know it's him. I want to see if I can hack into the bank and get better video—I want to see if he was there for a specific reason. And I want to hunt down where he's staying." Unless he'd skipped town, something she'd worry about if they couldn't find him.

Dylan's gaze darkened slightly. "What kind of man is he?"

"I...don't know how to answer that. On jobs, I trusted him to have my back. But two people Samara and I worked with on an operation are dead. And it appears he might have stolen a bunch of money. Apparently they couldn't prove he'd taken it. That didn't matter—he was fired. And now he's in Miami and we've both been shot at? I don't know. I don't like it. There isn't anything connecting him for sure, but hell, for all I know he's a target too. I simply want to talk to him."

"I can help. What bank did you get the video from?"

When she named the bank, he gave her a wry grin. "I own the building. So you won't have to do any hacking."

She blinked in surprise and grinned. "Good, because I suck at hacking and I don't want to call in any favors yet."

"In case we need someone, I know a guy."

She lifted an eyebrow. "Really?"

"Technically it's a woman. But yeah, I know someone who can help us out if things get that far."

Evie didn't like the weird frisson of jealousy that sparked through her. Of course Dylan knew other women. He knew hundreds of other women. She was just being stupid and getting all caught up in her head. "I'm ready to get started on this now, if you are," She knew she was putting him out by asking for these favors. Especially since he owed her nothing and had multiple businesses to run.

"I don't like the thought of you leaving my place. Not after what happened."

"I'll be going in disguise." There was more than one disguise in her stash bag and it would be easy enough to alter her appearance. She wondered if Dylan or his guy had dug through her things, then immediately dismissed the thought. Of course he had, she realized. And he had every right to. She'd brought danger into his house.

Dylan simply nodded. "Fine. I'm going to call the off-site security place where the videos are dumped. They can send me anything we want but I'm guessing you want to look at things in person?"

She nodded. "Give me fifteen minutes. I just need to gear up."

He nodded, his green eyes watchful. "Do you need to make a stop to see your brother or family?"

She'd spent the morning with her family and she couldn't just sit around doing nothing. "I just talked to my mom. Evan still won't see anybody. He's been quite adamant about it in fact. Jackass," she muttered, angry with her older brother. Angry and afraid for him. It wasn't healthy to keep pushing family away.

"I'm sorry you're dealing with all this."

Her too. "I just want to help Samara at least. I feel like maybe..."

"What?"

She paused even as she told herself to keep her mouth shut. But her brain wouldn't listen to her. Dylan had always been more than just a lover. He'd been a friend and an incredible sounding board. Because he'd truly listened. Not just waited for her to finish so he could start talking. "I don't know. I feel like if I can help her, I'll be doing some good right now." She should leave, but instead she found herself stepping farther into his office. She collapsed on one of his chairs and rubbed both hands over her face. "I feel so useless where my brothers are concerned. I can't do anything for Evan. And I can't find Ellis to help him—and I've tried. I hate not being able to help my family." She'd done so much for her country—for strangers—and now she couldn't help the two people who meant everything to her.

He surprised her by crouching down in front of her and taking her hands in his. "You're doing everything you can. And Evan will come around. He's had a traumatic experience. You know he won't shut you guys out forever."

She did know that. And for some stupid reason she found her gaze locked on Dylan's full lips as he crouched in front of her, comforting her. In that moment she felt like a jerk. He was trying to be a decent guy and all she could think about was kissing him, tasting him, maybe forgetting the insanity of her life right now. Yeah, because that would be so *fair* to him. She couldn't do that to him. Ugh, she sucked.

She snapped her gaze away, clearing her throat. "You're right, of course." She abruptly stood, needing distance from him in that moment.

What the hell was she thinking, getting all vulnerable in front of him? She walked to the door, her movements stiff and stilted.

"You're going to tell me all your secrets," Dylan murmured, his low, sexy tone surprising her. And...knocking her off-balance.

She started to tell him that he was wrong, that she would never tell him all her secrets. But the words stuck in her throat.

With a trembling hand, she yanked open the office door and practically ran from him.

What the hell had just happened? She couldn't tell him her secrets. If she did, it would be the final nail in her coffin.

He wouldn't help her, wouldn't look at her with flashes of interest or lust. No, he would loathe her.

And...she couldn't stand the thought of that.

CHAPTER NINE

"I need to stop by Ellis's house now," Evie said as they headed away from the security place. She'd gone inside the nondescript, four-story building with Dylan—looking nothing like herself. Wearing a platinum blonde wig, square-framed glasses, colored contacts, and a bit of theater-grade makeup, she'd changed her appearance enough that if anyone was searching for her using facial recognition software, they wouldn't find her. It was why she'd gone with the particular wig. The sharp bob covered her ears so they wouldn't be picked up on any cameras. And blonde went with her coloring. Not that any of that mattered now since the trip had been a bust and they were no closer to finding Seamus.

"Sure. What's going on?"

"I got an alert on my phone. I have the app for his alarm system on there and it said there was some movement on one of the doors. The alarm system was turned off, however." And she didn't like that.

Dylan gave her a sharp look. "You think it's him?"

"Could be. I'm not sure why he'd go back to his house. I just wish he would reach out to me," she muttered. Evie had been trying not to think too much about Ellis. She loved him. She knew he could take care of himself, but it didn't alleviate her fear for him, especially with everything else going on.

"He's not going to reach out to you and compromise your safety." Dylan's voice was sure. "You want to talk about that case? I only know what the news has said. That he killed an undercover DEA agent he was working with and went on the run... Something I don't believe."

Closing her eyes, she shook her head as he took a left turn. "No. Not now. But thank you." Maybe she would talk about it later, but it was too painful to focus on.

"I know you won't tell me who you used to work for—though I have my guesses. Can you at least tell me why you started working for them?"

She opened her eyes and glanced at him. "You're probably going to laugh."

"Try me." His tone was dry.

"I wish I could say it was something noble like I wanted to serve my country... Though eventually that's what it turned into. I'm proud of what I've done. But honestly, it sounded really cool and I wanted nothing to do with my parents' way of life. Now that I'm older I understand I was just being a spoiled jackass. They give a lot to our community but...I didn't want any part of their money. I wanted to carve out my own identity."

She cleared her throat before continuing.

"In college I was recruited because of my aptitude for languages and my social skills, really. I'm able to pretty much blend in anywhere, relatively speaking. And it sounded like a whole lot of fun. I would get to see the world, learn new skills and kick ass occasionally." Since she'd grown up with two older brothers, she knew all about roughhousing, and she'd taken to martial arts like a fish to water. When she'd been recruited, she hadn't wanted to get stuck in Miami working for one of her father's companies. It had all seemed so stifling and boring at the time and the CIA had offered her a whole new world. So she'd jumped on it.

He nodded as he looked back at the road. "I get that."

"You're a bit more noble than me," she said, grinning. She knew Dylan had joined the Marines because of a sense of duty and honor. That was just the kind of guy he was.

"We've both still served our country. The reasons don't really matter in the end." Dylan was ever the pragmatist.

Something she liked about him. He was so damn well-adjusted. His own family was similar to hers, and he'd gone off and joined the military—and fought in multiple war zones. Sometimes when she looked at him, she saw the warrior looking back at her. He might have left the Marines, but the Marines hadn't left him. It was probably why he was such a shark in business. She lifted a shoulder.

"Why did you quit? Why are you back in Miami?"

That wasn't something she was willing to answer right now. "That's a story for another day," she said as she pulled up another one of the outdoor security feeds from her brother's place on her phone. Still, nothing. "I don't see any movement on the cameras outside." Now she wished there were cameras inside. Damn it. She didn't like not knowing who was inside her brother's house. And she was afraid that by the time they got there, whoever it was would be gone.

If it was Ellis and she'd missed him...ugh.

Evie was glad that the sun had already set as Dylan parked a few houses down from her brother's house. The darkness garnered more cover and she had a feeling they were going to need it. They weren't in the same vehicle they'd been in when they'd been shot at. Now they were in an SUV with bullet-resistant everything. "How do you want to do this?" she asked.

"I want to call the cops," he said dryly.

She shot him a glare. "What if it's Ellis inside?" She would be the worst sister ever if she ended up inadvertently calling the cops on him. When Dylan didn't respond, she continued. "I'm thinking that we can either go in together or I can take the back door and you can take the front door. Or vice versa. It doesn't matter." They were both armed and trained.

"All right. We'll do it your way." He got out of the vehicle, his movements quiet as they strode down the sidewalk. "It's weird talking to you like this, knowing you've got a hell of a lot of training."

"I know." She pushed back the prick of pain in her chest. "I knew you would never like this version of me."

He frowned, his fingers gently skimming over her forearm for an instant before he pulled back. "I didn't say that. Just that it was weird. I like this version of you too." He looked as if he wanted to say more, but held back.

Glancing away, she cleared her throat. They were close now. Had to stay sharp and not think about how she loved every single version of Dylan. "So what's it gonna be?"

"We go in with me taking point."

She narrowed her gaze at him as they reached Ellis's neighbor's front yard. "Because I'm a woman?"

"No. Because I care about you."

Damn it. "How about we go in at the same time? You go high, I'll go low."

He definitely wanted to argue, she could see that from the tense line of his jaw, but he simply nodded as they casually strolled up the neighbor's driveway when Evie pointed in that direction.

Moving quickly, they hurried up the driveway. Instead of making their way up to the front door, like a visitor would do, they kept going along the side of the gray and blue cottage.

When she'd moved into Ellis's house, she'd learned the layout of most of his neighbors' yards. She'd done far too much recon for a normal person but she liked to know her surroundings at all times. "Part of the fence needs mending," she whispered. "We won't even need to jump it."

Dylan nodded, and when she pointed out the opening in the seam of the fence he slid through first.

She quickly followed, careful to avoid the floodlights.

Anticipation built inside her. What if it was *Ellis* inside? She missed her brother so much and wanted to pull him into a giant hug. More than that, she wanted to clear his name.

"I see movement." Dylan's voice was low as he nodded at the upstairs window.

The lamp was on—and she hadn't left it on. A hint of a shadow shifted behind the roman shades. "That's Ellis's bedroom," she whispered back.

Dylan nodded, and after a quick scan of the backyard they hurried toward the back door.

Evie withdrew her weapon, Dylan doing the same. He was right—it was weird to be here with him like this in operator mode. But she also kind of liked it. Liked being able to be herself at least.

Eyes on the door, she counted down before she gently twisted the knob. The handle easily turned, swinging open. So someone had either picked the lock or they had a key. They hadn't reset the alarm system either, which was good for them.

She kept her weapon out as they swept into the kitchen.

Empty.

Dylan quietly shut the door behind them.

She could hear the faint shuffles of someone moving around upstairs. She wasn't sure if it was more than one person.

They hurried through the house, briefly sweeping each dark room as they passed by it until they got to the stairs. Though she wanted to go first, Dylan stepped in front of her to take the lead as they hurried up the stairs.

She heard the faint sound of a male cursing. The sound was too quiet for her to distinguish whether it was her brother.

Heart racing, she eased down the hallway toward Ellis's bedroom. The door was cracked open, muted light spilling out onto the hardwood floors of the hallway.

Dylan motioned that he was going in first and there was no way she could argue with him right now.

Dylan tapped the door open with his foot, weapon up.

Evie was right behind him as they went through the doorway.

"Hands up!" Dylan snapped at the guy wearing a ski mask.

Evie knew immediately it wasn't her brother. The man's build was too small. Before the guy could respond, there was a shuffling behind her, the sound so faint she might have missed it as the guy in the ski mask lunged at them.

Turning, weapon still in hand, she jerked backward as a fist came straight at her face.

Shit. There were two of them.

She ducked, barely avoiding the blow from the meaty fist as Dylan grappled with the other guy. She collided with the door in her attempt to avoid getting punched. She was worried about Dylan but knew he could take care of himself.

The second guy rushed her, body-slamming her against the door. He was too damn heavy, pinning her arm in place. She released the weapon, cringing as it clattered to the floor. But she needed her hands free.

Adrenaline pumping, she lashed out, slamming her fists into the middle of his chest.

The guy cried out, releasing her. Without giving him a chance to recover, she landed four quick blows—to his throat and gut—even as she kicked at his inner knee.

It was clear the guy had no training. He was huge, but slow.

"Bitch!" he shouted as he swung at her again. "You're gonna pay for that!"

This time she wasn't as quick and his fist grazed her jaw. Twisting her head to the side, she barely felt it as she nailed him in the balls with her knee. She inwardly grinned as he fell to the floor. Then she jammed her knee up into his nose for one final blow. Blood spurted everywhere as she slammed him to the floor.

She wrenched his arms behind his back as he moaned out in pain, making pathetic blubbering sounds.

An instant later Dylan was beside her with a phone cord, wrapping it quickly around the guy's wrists. She glanced up to see the other guy, knocked out cold, flat on his back.

She whipped off the ski mask of the guy underneath her but didn't recognize him. He had thick, dark hair, brown eyes—and a broken, bloody nose. He glared at her, muttering curses about how she was going to pay for this.

"Now we're calling the cops," Dylan said.

She nodded because he was right. "Shut up *now*," she snapped at the whiner.

The guy's dark eyes went wide but he stopped.

She looked at Dylan. "Call them, but I'm taking their fingerprints first." Reaching into a little zipper pocket at the bottom of her cargo pants, she pulled out a device she'd swiped when she'd left the Agency. Some habits definitely died hard.

He lifted an eyebrow at the high-tech device but didn't comment as she scanned in both men's finger-prints.

As Dylan called Detective Duarte, she bound the un-conscious guy's hands and started scanning the array of papers the two men had been digging through.

They'd busted open the safe in her brother's closet and emptied out what looked like one of her brother's filing cabinets from his office. She knew that nothing of importance was in the safe. The DEA had seen to that weeks ago. And hell, she'd done a scan of the house her-self and found nothing.

Of course she didn't know what the heck she was looking for so if there was something that could help her brother, she could have missed it.

"He's on his way," Dylan said a few minutes later. He paused, looking at her, then motioned that she should step out into the hallway with him.

"What?"

"Your…appearance. How are you going to play this?"

Hell. "Stay with these guys. I'll take care of it." While she'd done nothing wrong by wearing a disguise, it was better not to stand out to Detective Duarte in any way. She hurried to the bedroom she'd been staying in and stripped off the wig and glasses. Then she made quick work of the makeup and pulled on a ball cap. Not perfect, but it would have to do.

She was going to find out who the heck these guys were. And if they had anything to do with her brother's trumped-up murder charge, she was going to get some answers.

CHAPTER TEN

"You're not very good at being patient, are you?"
Dylan murmured. Both he and Evie had been
waiting in Carlito's office for over two hours with no
word from the detective. He was frustrated just like her,
but she'd been pacing like a caged tiger.

"Normally I am. Not tonight." Sighing, she sat in the
chair next to him, but on the edge of it, not fully relax-
ing.

She was wearing a ball cap with a hockey team's logo
on it, her long, dark hair tied back in a ponytail. All her
muscles were pulled taut, her forearms tense as she held
on to the edge of the seat. He could practically see the
wheels in her head turning.

"He'll see us when he's done." Dylan assumed Carlito
was questioning the two guys from Ellis's place right
now. The detective had dumped them in here, then disappeared.

Evie stood and started pacing. Again.

He rolled his shoulders once. "You get any hits on
their fingerprints?"

She paused, glanced at the door, then nodded. "I'll
tell you about it once we're out of here," she murmured.

He doubted that Carlito's office had listening devices
but...she was right. Before he could respond, the detective opened the door, his gray eyes flashing in anger as

he shut the door behind him. *Uh oh.* Dylan knew whatever the man had to say wasn't good. He straightened in his seat.

"I'm sorry you guys had to wait so long."

"What's wrong?" Evie asked, sensing the same anger rolling off Carlito.

The detective sighed and leaned against the edge of his desk. "The DEA took them out of our custody. Said they've got jurisdiction. I fought it with my chief but there's nothing we could do about it."

"The DEA and not the FBI?" Evie's question was neutral enough, but Dylan was pretty sure he understood why she was asking.

The FBI were the ones investigating Ellis Bishop's alleged crimes. Because of the nature of the crime and suspect—a DEA agent—it would have been a conflict of interest for the DEA to investigate their own agent… But now the DEA was taking two men into custody who'd broken into Ellis's house? That surprised Dylan too.

"Yep. DEA," Carlito confirmed.

Dylan watched as Evie's hands balled into fists, but just as quickly she shoved out a breath. "Okay, then. Do you need us for anything else?"

Carlito blinked once in surprise, maybe at her quick acquiescence. "At this point, no. Though…I do find it interesting that you were both armed when you entered your brother's house." He lifted an eyebrow, looking between the two of them.

Dylan stood. "We both have concealed weapons permits and Evie received an alert on her phone that someone was inside. Why wouldn't we go in armed?" And that was all he was going to say about that. They'd given their statements.

"You should have called the police." Carlito's tone was admonishing.

Dylan simply shrugged. "We're done here. Thank you for your help." He took Evie's elbow, glad that she leaned into him.

"Yes, thank you for your help, detective." Evie's voice was almost too polite as they headed toward the door.

Carlito simply sighed. "Call me if you need anything...and call us if you're in trouble," he muttered as they stepped out into the hallway.

"You let that go quickly," Dylan murmured.

"If the DEA took them, there's nothing we can do about that. I'm not going to waste time arguing with a Miami detective about it. He certainly can't do anything about it."

"They showed up awfully fast."

"Yeah." Evie frowned at that. Then her frown deepened as they stepped into the lobby to find Leo waiting for them. "What's he doing here?"

"Driving us home." After tonight Dylan was damn sure increasing their security.

Leo spoke for the first time as he steered them out of the Miami PD parking lot. "Trouble seems to follow you around, Ms. Bishop." His tone was admonishing...judgmental.

"Leo." Dylan's voice was sharper than he'd intended. But he didn't want his head of security—his friend—giving Evie any grief right now. She'd hoped to find her brother tonight and instead they'd run across what was definitely not a simple breaking and entering.

Leo met his gaze in the rearview mirror for a moment before he faced the road.

"He's not wrong," Evie murmured, laying her head on his shoulder.

The action took him by surprise and her too it seemed, because she jolted up, looking almost embarrassed before she pulled her cell phone out. He wasn't shy about watching who she texted either. Very clearly an FBI agent—and she told the woman what had happened tonight with the DEA.

"Who is that?" he asked, motioning to her phone. "The agent in charge of Ellis's investigation?"

"No, another one. She's running the investigation into the bombing. But I know she'll make sure the right people find out about this."

"You think the FBI doesn't know yet?" he asked as she slid her phone back into her pocket.

"I don't know who those guys were." *Yet* was the unspoken word. "But I find it hard to believe the FBI would let the DEA take some guys breaking into the house of someone they have an active criminal investigation on. No...they won't be happy at all."

Dylan wasn't either. Not about any of this. His world had been upended since the moment he'd met Evie but this was a whole other ballgame.

For some reason, he didn't mind the chaos. Not as long as Evie was in his life. But he wanted to know the real her. All of her.

* * *

Dylan froze in the entrance to his private gym. After checking on Cooper—and finding him shamelessly dozing on Samara's bed—he'd come looking for Evie and now he'd found her. She was pounding away on a punching bag, wearing a black sports bra and little black shorts. He didn't think she was aware of him, because her focus was solely on destroying the punching bag. At ten p.m. it was late to be working out, but he understood her need to release frustration.

Her jet-black hair was pulled back in a braid and sweat rolled off her arms and down her back as she hit the bag over and over. Her muscles flexed with each movement, her arms and legs lean and toned. This was the real Evie Bishop. This driven, focused woman. A woman who was hunting for the truth.

He took a small step inside and she must have heard or seen him out of the corner of her eye.

Turning, she let her hands drop. "Hey."

He crossed the distance between them, fighting the urge to touch her, to cup her face, to take her onto the mat right here. To kiss her senseless. "How are you feeling?"

She stripped off the gloves and hung them neatly on the hook by the towels. Then she grabbed a white towel and ran it over her face and head. "Frustrated. Angry." Her jaw tightened once as she wrapped the towel around her neck, holding on to the ends as she watched him. "I can't find Seamus. I can't find my brother. I don't even know if Seamus is the one targeting us. I have a whole lot of unknowns and limited resources. And pounding on this punching bag is doing nothing to alleviate my stress. I want to find whoever bombed Evan, and beat their head in." Her voice rose slightly as she continued. "I also want to kick the ass of whoever set up Ellis. And I really want to know who shot my friend and took a shot at me." Her expression was hard, her hands in tight balls again, but she took a deep breath, then expelled it before sitting on the bench next to the towels. "Sorry, you don't want to hear me whine."

"It's not whining. And I might be able to help you on the Seamus front. I set up an appointment with the friend of mine I told you about. The hacker. I gave her the details on Seamus we got from the security feeds. She's doing a search for him." He hadn't had much to give his friend but the images should be enough.

Her head snapped up as she stood. "You did that without telling me?"

"Yes." They hadn't had time to talk about it since leaving the security office so he'd simply taken care of it.

"It's dangerous to run his information. Did you think about that?"

He narrowed his gaze at her tone. "No. I didn't think about that. Because I'm a dumbass."

"That's not what I said."

"You're implying it," he snapped. "Of course I took precautions. The woman I asked is a friend. I would never put her in danger."

"A friend?"

Was that jealousy in her tone? Frowning, he took a step closer. "Does it matter?"

"Nope." She started to walk away from him but he reached out, grabbing her forearm.

"She is just a friend." He tugged her closer, not caring that she was sweaty. "A very happily married one."

She placed a hand on his chest, gave a weak push. "You still should have asked me. I don't want to put anyone in danger."

He tugged her even closer. "Yeah, well I didn't." And he wasn't sorry. Evie needed the info, needed to find this guy. And he was damn sure going to help.

"What do you want from me?" she whispered when he still didn't let go.

He wasn't sure why she was even asking since he hadn't said anything. Maybe the question was rhetorical because he was still holding her arm. Regardless, the answer was that he wanted everything. The truth, the real her, which he was only just starting to see—and he liked what he saw. His gaze dipped to her mouth, and when she licked her lips a slight groan escaped. *Hell.* He shouldn't want her so much, shouldn't be so obsessed with her. But he couldn't help it—he'd never gotten over her. And he wasn't sure he ever would. She was in his blood.

He wasn't certain who moved first but suddenly they were kissing, his tongue teasing against hers as she wrapped her entire body around him. Her legs tightened around his waist as she dug her fingers into his shoulder.

They needed a flat surface. Now. The mat would do. It wouldn't take long to strip her down. All he would have to do was slide his hand down the front of her little shorts, cup her mound and slip a finger inside. Would she be wet for him?

He hoped so because he was already rock-hard for her. Seeing her working out turned him on. Knowing she was in his house, under his roof, turned him on. *Everything* she did turned him on. It was beyond reason.

But that was just the way it was and he was going to have to accept it. Because he didn't think there was another woman for him other than Evie Bishop. She was his not-so-secret addiction.

At the sound of someone clearing their throat, they both froze. He tore his gaze to the doorway, glared at one of his security guys. "What?" he snapped out. Something better be on fire.

"A detective is here to see you. Detective Duarte. He's got something important to tell you." The man wasn't looking directly at them, but slightly off to the side as if he wanted to be anywhere but here.

"Give me ten minutes," he growled.

Evie let her legs drop from around him and he bit back another growl. "We've got to talk to him," she said, immediately putting some distance between them.

"Not sure why he didn't just call." Dylan rolled his shoulders once. They'd been moments away from both being naked, from him being deep inside her. Maybe the interruption was for the best. For...reasons.

Evie grabbed a dry T-shirt and tugged it over her head. "I'll shower after we talk to him."

He frowned at her. "You want to put on different bottoms?"

She glanced down at herself, then looked up at him and frowned. "I can. Why?"

He didn't say anything, but looked at the shorts again. They didn't cover anything. Some caveman part of him didn't like her showing off so much skin. Which he *knew* was ridiculous but he was ridiculous where she was concerned.

She gave him a strange look, but grabbed a pair of long jogging pants and tugged them on over her skin-tight shorts. "Let's get this over with."

Dylan and Evie found Duarte waiting in the foyer, hands shoved in his pants pockets.

He straightened when he saw them. "I could've just called but I wanted to tell you in person. I was headed home when I got a call from my boss. The two guys who were taken into custody by the DEA were both killed during transport."

Evie let out a low curse as Dylan rubbed a hand over his face. If the two guys were dead, there wasn't a threat of them coming back and trying to get revenge on him and Evie for interrupting their B&E and getting them arrested. But he guaranteed those two guys had been working for someone. Someone who had decided they needed to die.

"How were they killed?" she demanded before Dylan could ask the same thing.

"Another prisoner. Not sure how they managed to sneak a weapon on board but they did. That's all I know—except the prisoner who killed them is dead now too." He looked as if he wanted to say more, but then cleared his throat. "I thought you deserved to know," he finished.

Thankfully the detective didn't want to make small talk so he left after a short goodbye.

"This is bullshit," Evie muttered as soon as the door shut behind him. "That's a setup if I've ever heard of one. Whoever set my brother up has to be involved in this. Involved in killing those guys. It's gotta be a dirty DEA agent because no one else would be able to smuggle a weapon in during transport. And now that prisoner is dead too? No way." She let out a growl of frustration then turned and left, stalking away from Dylan and down the hallway.

His instinct was to follow after her but he let her go. She needed to work out whatever was going on in her head and he was going to reach out to some more contacts. She'd run the information from the fingerprints on her device and he had their names. Soon, he would find out who those two guys had been. He might not be hacker-level like his friend Lizzy Caldwell, but he would do some searches of his own.

They were going to get to the bottom of this mess. He was going to find whoever had shot at Evie and her friend—and then he wanted straight answers from Evie.

She wanted him as much as he wanted her. Yet she'd left him. And he didn't buy that it was simply because of her former job. They still could have made things work even if she'd been working undercover. People did that every day. There was more to her leaving and he would find out what it was.

CHAPTER ELEVEN

Evie stepped away from Dylan's bedroom door then pivoted, turned back and raised her hand to knock. Then she repeated the process three more times, never following through.

What the hell was she doing? She shouldn't be here. Hell, she wasn't even sure why she was here other than it was three in the morning and she couldn't sleep.

She'd processed the fingerprints of the two men from her brother's house, and while she knew their names, she didn't know nearly enough about who they were. It didn't matter that they were dead. She was going to find out who they'd been working for and trace it back to whoever had set up her brother. But first she needed to figure out who wanted Samara dead.

In that vein, she'd been combing over old operation files she still had access to, trying to find out if Seamus had any assets he might be using here in Miami. She'd found a couple of potential hits, so if he was in contact with them, searching them out would be her next move. Because it stood to reason he would reach out to assets.

Damn it, she shouldn't be outside Dylan's room. No, she needed to go back to her room. But he was probably inside, naked.

When her phone buzzed in her pocket, she pulled it out and read the text. *Are you going to stay out there all night or come in?*

She blinked in surprise and looked around the hallway, but didn't see any cameras. Opening his door, she stepped inside. Cooper looked up from the end of the bed, his big brown eyes sorrowful before he made a sort of snuffling sound. Then he crossed his paws over each other and laid his head back down.

Dylan was in bed, propped up against his pillow, laptop in his lap, and of course the sexy man was shirtless. His ab muscles clenched and tightened as he shifted slightly and she flashed back on that kiss they'd shared. He hadn't cared that she'd been all sweaty from her workout. Nope, Dylan had never cared about stuff like that. He was a raw, sensual man. Warmth flooded her as she watched him.

She leaned against the doorframe. "How did you know I was outside?"

"It was a guess. Saw the shadow of your feet moving back and forth... And Cooper whined a couple times." He moved his laptop to the side. "Is Samara okay?"

"Yeah, she's sleeping." Which was good. Her friend needed it. "I don't know why I'm here."

He gave her an unreadable look then moved the laptop to the night table. As he did, Cooper jumped off the bed. The dog shot them a baleful look before trotting out of the room, no doubt in search of treats.

Sighing, she shut the door behind her and got into bed next to him but didn't get under the covers. Because yeah, that somehow made this less intimate. She inwardly rolled her eyes at herself. "Leo is right. I'm just bringing trouble to your doorstep," she said, even as she settled against the fluffy king-sized pillow. His familiar masculine scent teased her, reminding her of the many times they'd shared this very bed together.

Dylan moved closer and wrapped his arm around her shoulders.

She must be a masochist because she leaned into him, laying her cheek against his chest as if this was a normal occurrence. As if they hadn't been broken up for months and she hadn't shown up on his doorstep little more than a day ago desperate for help.

"Leo is good at his job. And I don't care what he thinks about you."

"Why are you being so nice to me?"

"News flash. I like you."

She snorted against him but didn't look up. "I don't know why. I can be moody and prickly according to Samara." How could he like the real her?

He laughed lightly, the rumble vibrating through her. "Are you under the illusion that you were sweet and acquiescent when we were together? Because you weren't. You're a passionate and sometimes prickly woman. I don't care. I can be a moody jackass."

"You say the sweetest things," she murmured, making him laugh.

His huge room was quiet, with the faint sound of ocean waves in the distance. But the floor-to-ceiling drapes were pulled over the wall of windows, making it seem like they were in a cocoon. As if nothing else existed.

She knew that this moment with him wouldn't last but she was going to take this calm between them. She was going to grasp this stolen moment with the man she still loved but could never have. "I can't turn my brain off. I'm just so worried about everything. I've never…it's never been like that for me before. I've always been able to compartmentalize things."

"You can't compartmentalize when it comes to your family." He stroked his fingers down her spine in a gentle rhythm she'd missed.

She'd worn a simple black tank top and loose flannel pants with pockets to sleep in. Definitely not what she used to wear when she'd gone to bed with him. No, then she'd worn nothing. This was different, but nice.

"How are you able to take off time from work?" She knew he was busy but he'd stepped up to help her in a big way.

"I pay a lot of people to do their jobs well so I don't have to micromanage. I'm keeping in touch with the people I need to keep in touch with though. Nothing needs my direct attention right now."

She sighed, snuggling up closer to him. Being next to him made her feel safe, something she knew was an illusion. Nonetheless, she felt that way with him. As if nothing could touch them. She wished that was true, that they had more time together.

"We were on the news, you know," he continued.

Frowning, she sat up. "What do you mean?" She'd been so focused on researching Seamus and other things that she hadn't been watching the local news. It was usually bullshit anyway and she got tired of seeing the same media talking heads discussing the explosion at her brother's building. She knew what had happened and it cut deep every time she saw a recap of it.

"It was just a quick recording of us. Someone must have caught us leaving the police station."

Damn. She'd only been with him for a little over twenty-four hours. "What was the news about?"

"Your brothers, mainly. Lots of speculation about the Bishop companies and stock. Questions about the bombing, questions about Ellis being wanted for murder. Then gossip wanting to know if you and I were back together." His tone was dry.

"Ah," she said, laying her head back against his chest. "I hope associating with me doesn't hurt your business."

He actually laughed. "Don't worry about that."

"I miss you," she whispered. She probably shouldn't admit that to him, shouldn't make herself vulnerable. But he deserved it. He deserved much more than she could give him right now. He'd gone above and beyond what a friend, let alone an ex, should do. And they'd never been simply friends anyway. She'd hurt him, yet here he was, stepping up.

He shifted so quickly he took her off guard when he pinned her underneath him. "I miss you too. So why did you leave me?" His green eyes flared with anger. Gone was the calm man she knew so well.

"I told you."

"What you told me was bullshit. You thought I wouldn't like 'this version' of you. You told me you didn't want to be stuck in Miami. Then you moved right back here months after you left. If you didn't want to be with me, that was all you had to say. Not come up with a pack of lies."

"I do want to be with you." Her voice trembled. "But it would never work out."

"Why not?"

She pressed her lips together, not willing to tell him everything. Not yet. Maybe never. She wasn't noble like him. She was terrified of his rejection. She could admit her own weakness. Dylan Blackwood.

"You're not going to answer me?" he pressed.

"No," she whispered. She tensed, expecting him to kick her out then. She wasn't giving him the answers he deserved.

To her surprise, however, he crushed his mouth to hers, stealing her breath and her heart.

She ate at his mouth, kissing him in a frenzy. This kiss brought back a flood of naked memories. Him pressing her up against his shower wall. Her riding him on this very bed. His big, strong hands tracing every inch of her naked body... Yep, they both needed to be naked. Right now. Hell, ten minutes ago.

Frenetic energy hummed through her as she shoved at his lounge pants. He wouldn't be wearing anything underneath if things hadn't changed. She didn't tear her mouth from his as she managed to shove them down his long, muscular legs. More memories flashed in her mind, of her touching him everywhere, learning every inch of his finely honed body.

Reaching between their bodies, she wrapped her fingers around his erection and stroked once, groaning as she did. God, she'd missed him.

He moaned into her mouth, sliding his hands under her tank top, cupping her breasts with his big, callused hands. "Clothes off now," he growled against her mouth, his words uneven.

She could definitely handle that. In record time she stripped her clothes off, desperate to be skin to skin with him.

"I'm still on the pill," she rasped out as he settled between her legs again. The feel of him on top of her, the feel of his cock thick and heavy between them, was so familiar. Then she froze, realizing that he'd probably been with other women in the last six months. "I'm still clean," she said carefully. Some of the energy and heat started to dim as reality set in.

"Me too," he snapped. "And I haven't been with anyone else, if that's what you're thinking."

Relief washed over her, a soothing balm to her frayed nerves. "Me neither." It was as if something inside her snapped free as she leaned up, meeting his mouth with hers.

The kiss quickly turned savage as their mouths clashed. They were both so hungry for each other, the energy rolling off him mirroring her own.

How had she lived without him for six months? Hell, how had she lived before him? He was this bright, beautiful swath of color in her world, and once she'd lost him it had been like losing part of herself. She'd never recovered. Instead she'd kept on living her life with a hole inside her.

He reached between their bodies, cupping her mound and sliding two fingers inside her in a smooth, practiced motion.

Her inner walls tightened around him as she arched her hips, rolling up against him. She was soaked.

"Fuck," he growled against her mouth, his body vibrating with energy.

Then he shifted down her body, burying his face between her legs with no warning. Not that she needed it. And for some reason the action surprised her, though it shouldn't. He'd always been so raw and sensual.

Her inner walls tightened again, desperate to feel him inside her. But he was clearly going to take his time torturing her—in the best way possible.

He flicked his tongue against her slick folds and teased her clit mercilessly, bringing her right to the edge of climax in the way only he knew how. He'd learned her body long ago and he hadn't forgotten exactly what she liked. What she needed.

"Inside me, now." A not so quiet demand.

"Foreplay," he said as he shifted again, moving up her body and caging her in with his forearms. She loved the way his muscles bunched and flexed.

"Later. Need this now." She couldn't even get out a complete sentence, but only force out a few words past her tight throat. She grabbed him by the back of his neck, not that he needed the motivation.

He crushed his mouth to hers again as he settled his cock between the juncture of her thighs. Then he was inside her, thrusting, over and over.

She felt completely filled by him. In more ways than one. Right now was very dangerous for her heart. But it was hard to care as ribbons of pleasure flowed through her, as he thrust over and over, pushing her to the edge of sanity.

He reached between their bodies as she scored her nails down his back. And when he teased her clit with just enough pressure, it pushed her over the edge.

She was already on a tightrope and this was all it took to send her tumbling off. Her climax was fast and sharp.

"Evie!" He let go too, emptying himself inside her in long, hard strokes as she found her own release.

It felt as if her climax went on forever. She clung to him, unable to let go, too afraid of what would happen if she did. Part of her was terrified that this wasn't real, that she was just dreaming. Eventually she came back to herself, stroking her hands down his spine as she savored the simple act of touching him. It was a miracle she'd lived without him for so long.

He brushed his lips over hers even as he remained on top of her, still inside her. "I'm going to get all your secrets," he whispered, mirroring what he'd told her yesterday. "That hasn't changed."

In response, she kissed him again. He probably would get all her secrets. Because she was weak where he was concerned. And once he had them all, once he knew that she'd targeted him, that she'd used him, he would walk away. But he wouldn't be able to take her memories. No one could do that.

They were hers and she would keep them locked up tight forever.

E vie opened her eyes at a buzzing sound. She faintly
heard the sound of water running in the background and realized Dylan must be in the shower.

The buzzing continued. What time was it? Oh shit,
her phone. She jolted upright and started searching for
it. She found it on the floor with her discarded pajama
pants. It was only six in the morning so she hadn't slept
too long. Hell, they'd barely slept at all.

Blinking, she read the texts Samara had sent one after the other.

Where are you?
I'm in your room and you're not here.
Your bed is made. Did you leave?

Crap. She quickly texted Samara back. *I'm in the gym.
I'll meet you in your room in just a minute.*

She tugged on her pajamas and hurried out of the
room. It didn't take her long to reach Samara's bedroom. Thankfully she didn't run into any of Dylan's security guys—though she was pretty sure they were all
outside anyway.

She reached Samara's room as her friend stepped out
of Evie's bedroom.

Her friend looked her up and down then snorted.
"The gym? Is that what we're calling it now?"

She felt her cheeks flush. It was too early for this
conversation. "Shut up," she muttered. "And what's up?"

"I should ask you that." Samara stepped into her room with Evie. "But I'll give you a reprieve for now. I couldn't sleep and thought I'd see if you'd found anything new."

"Not in the last three hours." She pulled out her phone and checked the apps she had synced with her computer just to be sure. "You've got everything I do." She'd copied Samara on all the information she'd found and vice versa.

"I'm getting sick of being cooped up. We need to hunt down those assets today."

Evie nodded. She'd already have done it if not for what had happened at her brother's house—and the subsequent visit to the police station. "I agree." She looked out the window onto the huge pool and back-yard. "I've been thinking about telling Dylan the truth," she said quietly.

Since Samara had been on the Jensen op, she knew how Evie had targeted Dylan for an invite. After Dylan had gotten her the introduction to Jensen, she was supposed to have ended things with Dylan—but she hadn't. The team hadn't been thrilled, but she'd pushed back. Samara had been the only one back then who hadn't given her grief.

"That's an interesting choice," her friend said, easing onto the bed and only wincing slightly. If it wasn't for the threat against her life, Evie was sure she'd be fine to leave Dylan's house.

BISHOP'S KNIGHT | 131

"It's pretty obvious we had sex a couple hours ago.
And it's more than just sex for me. Him too. I don't like
lying to him." It ate away at her insides.

Samara lifted a shoulder. "Technically you're not lying."

"I'm withholding information." And it was the same
thing. She wouldn't reason it away in her own head.
That would do a disservice to what she felt for him,
what they'd shared.

"Do what you've got to do, girl. Let's figure out
who's trying to kill us first. Then tell him."

"Okay," she said, pulling out her buzzing phone
again. Telling Dylan now wouldn't serve any purpose.
They needed to figure out who was after them, and
once they had...she would come clean. She wondered
who the hell would be calling her so early— Her heart
skipped a beat when she saw Evan's cell phone number.
She swiped her finger across the screen. "Hey!"

"Hey yourself," he said, his voice raspy and scratchy.

Tears sprang to her eyes as his familiar voice filled
the line. "I don't know what to say... Can I come see
you?"

"Yes. I want to see you as soon as possible."

Thank God. "I can be there in twenty minutes."

"Okay. I'll see you then." He disconnected before she
could respond.

"It's my brother," she said to Samara, heading for the
door.

"I'm going to figure out our plan of attack for today.
Let me know when you leave the hospital and we'll take

care of business." Samara had a familiar gleam in her eyes that said she was ready to kick ass.

She eyed her friend critically. "Are you up to driving around while we hunt these guys down?" They knew more than most how boring recon work could be. People thought being a spy was all glamorous but a lot of the time it meant sitting in a vehicle or some other spot, watching people. Boring as shit.

"I won't be able to kick in doors or anything, but I can still be your backup. My brain isn't broken."

"All right, then. I'll call you as soon as I leave the hospital."

She hurried back to Dylan's room and shut the door as he was stepping out of the bathroom. Steam billowed out after him. Of course he was naked, and any other time she would have savored the view—would have jumped him.

Before he could say anything, she said, "Evan called. He wants to see me. I have to go to the hospital."

"Give me five minutes to dress."

She simply nodded and hurried out of his room and back to her own. She wouldn't disrespect him by telling him he didn't need to come. She wanted him with her anyway. If she'd ever thought she'd gotten over him, stuff like this was why she never had. Probably never could. He was immediately offering to come with her because he knew how important it was.

After getting dressed in record time, they made it to the hospital by breaking a few traffic laws. But she didn't care.

She probably should have called Isla or her parents but figured they'd already seen Evan and she'd just get caught up when she arrived. Something had obviously changed for her brother since he'd decided to see everyone, and it was about damn time.

As she and Dylan made it to the waiting room, some of her adrenaline had eased. But not much. She felt as if she was on an op right now.

Her parents and Isla stood as she entered, both looking as exhausted as she felt. "I got a call from Evan asking me to come see him. I'm glad he finally changed his mind about seeing everyone."

"He called you?" Isla let out a little gasp, her face crumpling, and Evie realized they hadn't known Evan had called. *Oh...hell.* Dylan squeezed her hand once, a steady rock by her side.

Even her parents were surprised, hurt clear in her mother's pale blue eyes. Then her mom said, "At least he wants to see someone." There was no rancor in her tone, just sadness and a little relief.

Evie looked to Dylan, feeling helpless and awkward. This wasn't what she'd expected.

He simply kissed the top of her head and murmured, "Go see him. I'll be waiting."

She would think about the fact that he'd just kissed her in front of her parents later. Things had shifted between them last night. For now, she shoved the thought away. He would never trust her until she told him everything. She got that. And once she did, everything would be a moot point anyway.

Sloughing off those thoughts, she found the nurse on duty to let her in to see her brother.

She'd been expecting him to be in bad shape, but shock punched through her to see Evan in bed, surrounded by starch-white sheets, half his face bandaged with crisp white strips of cloth. Both his eyes were visible, though his left one was bloodshot and bruises ringed around it.

Even though she'd told herself to be strong, tears sprang to her eyes as she crossed the distance and took his hand in hers, being as gentle as if she was holding a kitten. She kissed his knuckles, grateful to be touching him. Grateful that he'd survived. "I'm so glad to see you." Her voice was raspy as she fought back emotion.

He squeezed her hand, his grip weak. "I'm glad to see you too."

"Why aren't you seeing Mom and Dad? Or Isla? She's hardly left the hospital since you were admitted. She's a mess, Evan." Maybe Evie should hold off on the questions but...she didn't understand.

Pain flickered in his eyes at the mention of his fiancée and he looked away for a moment. "Tell Isla to go home," he rasped out.

Frowning, she poured a glass of water from the table and handed it to him. Then she pulled a chair close to the edge of the bed, not wanting to get too close and jostle him. "I'm not telling her to do anything. She's been here, only leaving for her father's funeral and to take care of some personal things. She just wants to see you and she's wearing your ring. Why are you shutting her out? She loves you."

"I don't want her to see me like this. She shouldn't have to end up with someone like me."

She frowned; this wasn't like her brother at all. "What the hell does that mean?"

He motioned to his bandaged face. "She'll stick with me to the bitter end no matter what. No matter how bad the disfigurement is. I don't want her stuck with a monster."

Evie reined in the impulse to tell him that he was being a dumbass. She didn't want to give him too much grief, considering the trauma he'd been through. Evie would try to talk some sense into him later. For now, she wanted to be a calming presence. "First, you're not a monster. Second, is there anything you need? Food, books, anything."

"No. But I've been watching the news cycle the last twenty-four hours. What the hell is going on with our family? I saw that Ellis is wanted for murder, and now you're apparently back together with Dylan Blackwood. I know Ellis's situation is way more important, but seriously, what is happening? And what's happening with the investigation into the bombing?" He closed his eyes for a moment, his jaw tightening as he seemed to fight off a wave of pain. He had to be on some serious medication, but she knew her brother was probably only taking the bare minimum.

"Ellis didn't do it. And we're going to make sure he gets cleared. Once he finally stops running, we've got an expensive attorney waiting on retainer to defend him. That's all I know about him right now. Jackass hasn't reached out to any of us." And she was salty about it. "As far as the investigation into the bombing goes, I know the agent in charge and she's good at her job. I know they've got a few leads but I don't know more than that. I can hack into their system if you want. Well, I know someone who can."

He blinked then let out a startled laugh which sounded rusty. "No. Don't do that...yet."

She squeezed his hand again and just stared at him. "Everyone is so worried about you, Evan."

"I know. I hate being stuck in this hospital. I hate not being able to do anything for anyone."

"I know. But keeping Isla and our parents out isn't helping anything."

Jaw tight, he simply looked away from her. "Can you let it go?"

"Of course." Damn it, she would not push him right now. "Why did you let me come in?"

"I knew you would tell me the truth about every-thing."

She grinned at him. "You know me well. I'll keep you updated with everything. Oh, I almost forgot. Last night there was a break-in at Ellis's house. Two guys. And I ran their fingerprints." She told him everything that happened.

He let out a low whistle when she was done.

She continued. "There's more. It involves me." She'd always been close with her brothers so even though she had to leave out some details, she told Evan everything she could about what was going on with her and Dylan.

"Damn," he murmured.

"Damn indeed."

After a long moment, he closed his eyes, his expression turning pained. "I can't believe Douglas is dead."

She squeezed his hand tight at the mention of Isla's dad. "Yeah, I know. Isla's...taking things pretty rough, which is to be expected. But she's made of tough stuff." Evie cleared her throat. "She just needs her partner right now."

"Evie—"

"Okay, okay." After seeing that look of pain on Isla's face, Evie felt like a jerk for even being in here when she was out in the waiting room. "But once you're out of this room, I'm not holding back."

"That's fair," he murmured, his eyes starting to drift shut.

"Just get better." *Dear God, please.* She couldn't imagine a world without her big brother in it. Hell, both her brothers.

* * *

When Evie stepped back into the private waiting room, she braced herself to see Isla and the others. She hugged everyone, then focused on Isla. "We need to talk."

Thankfully her mom seemed to understand and grabbed her dad's hand, so her parents and Dylan quietly stepped out of the room.

"How is he?" Isla asked, dark circles under her eyes.

"As well as can be expected. He's...not doing well with what happened."

"He still doesn't want to see me." Her tone was flat. Devoid of spirit.

Evie shook her head, a swath of emotions pouring through her. "No, and I'm really sorry."

Isla straightened, her jaw going rigid. "I lost my father but I feel like I've lost Evan too. I don't understand why he won't see me." Confusion and pain mixed in her words and expression.

"He's been burned, and he said he doesn't want you to see him like that."

Isla frowned. "I don't understand why not. We're engaged. I *love* him."

Evie simply pulled her into a hug and held tight. The way Evan had been talking, it sounded as if he was ready to end things with Isla, but Evie definitely wasn't going to tell the other woman that. She just hoped her brother figured things out soon and came to his senses.

When she pulled back, she said, "You need to go home. I know my brother and so do you. He's not going to change his mind anytime soon. And you need to take care of yourself now. Get some sleep in your own bed. Take a shower in your own bathroom. Then come back here. But you need to go home for just a little bit and get distance from this place. You've lost a whole lot, Isla."

Isla rubbed a hand over her face, looking worse than Evie had ever seen her. "I know. I just... My place is mostly packed up right now. I've been planning to move in with Evan, but..."

Oh, hell. Evie hadn't even thought of that. "I can find a place for you to stay if you need. Dylan owns like a billion properties. I'm sure there are some that are vacant."

Isla gave her a ghost of a smile and shook her head, little wisps of red hair flying free. "I haven't sold my place... I'd been planning to rent it. But thank you for the offer. I'll just head back to my condo. I've got my cell phone if Evan decides to reach out to me." There was more than a hint of bitterness in her tone. "And I need to figure out what I'm going to do about my father's business."

Everything would fall to Isla now, and it wouldn't be easy. "Let me know if you need anything. And that's *not* a hollow offer. I know you're dealing with a lot."

Isla half-smiled again. "And so are you. Thank you for the offer though." Sighing, she stood and grabbed her Burberry bag and matching coat.

Evie hung back as the other woman stepped out, figuring that Isla would say goodbye to her parents as well. She wanted to march back into her brother's room and shake some sense into him but knew that wouldn't do any good. And she needed to focus on problems she could actually solve.

Beginning with hunting down Seamus any way she could. If he was targeting them, he was going to feel her wrath.

CHAPTER THIRTEEN

"So what happened in there?" Dylan asked as they headed out of the hospital parking lot.

Evie shook her head, looking miserable. "I feel like the biggest jackass for hurting Isla."

"You didn't hurt her." That was all on Evan right now. Dylan couldn't believe the man was rejecting Isla. The pain she was going through had been palpable, cutting through the air. And Dylan had seen those two together. There had been no doubt in his mind they were a solid pair.

"I know. But she's struggling. Her dad just died and now Evan won't see her. It's too much to comprehend. Those two have always been so damn tight. I thought their bond was indestructible." She sounded baffled.

Yeah, he had too. But he'd also thought when he proposed to Evie, she'd say yes. "People deal with trauma in different ways."

"I guess," she muttered, pulling out her phone. "Shit. Samara found Seamus. She said she's going to see him with or without us."

Dylan cursed under his breath. "I can keep her from leaving the house."

"Yeah, you can. That's called kidnapping. You gonna keep me locked down too?"

He shot her a sideways glance. Things had shifted between them after last night. Well, technically this morning. It felt like a lifetime ago, when in reality it had only been a few hours. Hell, she'd only barreled back into his life like a hurricane less than two days ago. He wasn't sure where she was at as far as they were concerned, and to be honest, he wasn't sure where he was at either. He knew he didn't want to let her go. But he also knew he couldn't be with her until she came clean with him about everything. That wasn't how he operated, and if they were going to have any kind of a future together, he needed to be able to trust her. To trust that what they had was real.

Before he could answer, his own phone rang. When he saw Lizzy Caldwell's name on the screen, he pressed the online car system. "Hey, you're on speaker. I'm with Evie."

"Hey," Lizzy said. "Nice to sort of meet you. Look, I found your guy, Seamus. And I can get in a lot of trouble for what I hacked."

"What does that mean?" Evie asked.

A short pause. "I'm giving you plausible deniability."

Next to him, Evie snorted. "Thanks."

"So where is he?" Dylan asked.

She rattled off an address, then said, "You didn't get this information from me. Also...I think he might have stolen a shitload of money from the government. He's up to something shady. Once I locked on to his image, I ran a few crosschecks and found two very short videos from surveillance footage of him talking to...not good people. The footage is from strip clubs and I'm not sure of the context of what's going on. Doesn't look good though. I can send you the files through an encrypted link."

"Thanks," Dylan said. "I owe you one."

"Yeah, you do. And I'm definitely going to collect." There was humor in her words but he didn't doubt the truth. Lizzy Caldwell dealt in favors. "Listen...just be careful. The men he seems to be involved with are into running drugs and cutting off the heads of their enemies—literally."

"Noted," he said.

Evie raised an eyebrow as they disconnected. "The address Lizzy gave us is the same Samara found."

"We'll pick her up, then." He knew Evie was going to hunt down this guy no matter what he did or said, and it wasn't as if they could call law enforcement. This Seamus hadn't done anything illegal that they knew of. Yet.

No matter what, Dylan was going to go into this armed and prepared.

He briefly thought of telling Leo what he was doing, but he wasn't dragging his security guys into any of this. What he and Evie were handling was personal. He paid his guys for personal security, not to risk their damn lives because of shit he dragged them into. So while he could ask...he wouldn't. They all had lives and families. If shit went haywire, this risk was on him. He couldn't let them get hurt because of his choices. "Are you going to change your appearance for this?"

She nodded, tugging on the bill of her ball cap. "Yeah. I hated going like this to the hospital but I didn't want to freak my parents out."

"Do your parents know what you do for a living—or what you did?"

Looking away, she shook her head. "No. Ellis does. And I think Evan has an idea, but he doesn't know specifics. He's...always been pretty pragmatic about things. Never really questioned me."

Well that was interesting that Ellis knew. But Ellis had been DEA, so Dylan supposed that made sense if she worked with his agency. Or another one. He had his suspicions of which one too.

* * *

"That's a pretty sweet drone," Samara said from the backseat of Dylan's SUV.

Evie agreed. He was expertly maneuvering the exceptionally quiet camera drone while she held the tablet for him.

They were two blocks away from the foreclosed mansion Seamus was supposedly staying at. The dark tint of the SUV was giving them enough privacy. The mansion had more or less fallen through the real estate cracks and was currently bank owned. But it hadn't been listed anywhere—yet. It was in some sort of limbo. Somehow Lizzy Caldwell had tracked him here.

Evie knew the woman was good even though she didn't know her personally. Just by reputation. She was pretty sure the CIA had tried to recruit Lizzy years ago. But she was a little older than Evie, so she wasn't certain. However, she was inclined to believe that the intel was good since Samara had gotten a hit from one of Seamus's old assets by tracking the guy's cell phone movements—to here.

"Finn just texted me and said you shouldn't be moving around," Dylan said to Samara from the driver's seat, barely glancing at his phone as he flew the drone.

Evie wasn't sure exactly how much this drone had cost, but she knew the model and they were incredibly quiet. This was the type of technology the CIA used. Evie shot him a sideways glance. "Did you tell Finn what we're doing?"

"Hell no. He'd never let me hear the end of it." His voice was distracted as he continued flying.

"Shift your tablet a little," Samara said. "It hurts too much to move."

"You were the one who wanted to come on this thing," Evie said even as she adjusted her position so Samara could see better.

"Doesn't mean I'm not in pain."

"You're a pain."

"Are you two always like this?" Dylan murmured, faint amusement in his voice.

"Yes," they said, practically in unison.

"Except normally Samara is stinking up our recon stations with freaking Cheetos and candy." Evie shuddered, glad she didn't have to endure the smell of Cheetos in an enclosed space.

"I don't see you complaining when I share my candy." Samara's voice was tart.

"Speaking of which…" She turned slightly to look at her friend. "Did you bring any candy?"

"Nothing. We were out of Cheetos and there's only healthy stuff at Dylan's." She mock shuddered.

"I'll work on that," he said dryly. "Hey, shift the tablet back toward me just a little." They were trying to get a bird's-eye view of the house without being spotted and this was the best way to do recon right now. There was a big wall in front of the mansion, though the gates weren't locked.

Still, this afforded them the smartest way to get eyes on Seamus.

Evie kept her gaze on the tablet even as she moved it for Dylan. "There's some light flickering in one of the top bedrooms."

"Jackpot." Dylan's expression was completely focused and intense. She really tried not to think about how he usually looked like this during sex.

"This place doesn't have any electricity, so he could be using a generator or candles." Evie thought it was a pretty smart way to lie low if needed. Since the place was in foreclosure there weren't any active electric or water services set up here. Which was great for a traitor who wanted to hide out. There would be no way to track any random bills to him here. "Damn, this was smart of him," Evie said, even as she wanted to punch Seamus in the face.

"No kidding," Samara agreed. "No easy way to track this bastard. Not really."

The image on screen shifted as the drone dipped lower, flying closer to the window with the light. Closer, closer…

"You're really good at this," Evie said to Dylan. "You use this for work?"

"Kinda. We use them to take aerial views of properties. But I got my nephew a drone for Christmas and ended up getting one for myself because they were so much fun. Mine is a bit more high-tech though."

She laughed at his response, surprised. "You really are just a big kid sometimes."

He glanced at her, taking his eyes off the screen for a moment, and flashed her a real smile, revealing a tiny little dimple she'd missed until now.

Her heart skipped a beat at the sight of it. *Keep it together, Bishop,* she ordered herself. *You will not notice Dylan as a sexual being during an operation.* Except…this wasn't an op. Not really. And she couldn't not notice how sexy the man was, especially since he was all focused and intense as he maneuvered the drone even lower. He got that concentrated look during sex—usually when he was trying to get her to come. Oh hell, did it just get hotter in here?

"Here we go." Dylan's tone changed as well as his body language. "I see movement inside."

They all watched as a man stepped out of a bathroom. He had a towel around his waist and she could see a small generator in the corner as the drone flew lower. There was an air mattress with a couple blankets tossed onto the bed. Thankfully the tech should be quiet enough that anyone inside the home wouldn't be able to hear the low buzz.

"It's definitely him," she said as he ran his hand over his damp hair, flexing his arm and revealing a familiar tattoo.

"I'm going to do one more sweep of the house." Dylan shifted the drone higher and out of view of the window.

"Good. Then we go in. I want to catch him off guard," Evie said.

"I want to punch him in the dick if he's the one who shot me," Samara snapped.

"You're staying in the SUV," Evie said. "And don't argue. We need someone to keep an eye out for us. You've got to be a lookout."

Samara growled but acquiesced. "I'm only doing this because I've been shot."

"I'm well aware," Evie murmured. Normally her friend would have been the first one kicking in doors.

* * *

"I just want to go on record as saying I don't like this," Dylan said as he and Evie approached the house from the west, using the shadows of the falling darkness and the neighbor's overgrown trees to infiltrate the property. She had a short, bobbed, auburn wig on under her ball cap, covering her ears and half her face.

"You guys have got this," Samara said through their earpieces.

Despite having worked in the corporate world for a while, it only felt nominally strange to be using earpieces and infiltrating a place with weapons. Some habits were ingrained. It was weird, however, he thought for the tenth time, to see Evie holding a weapon as if it was part of her body. She was no longer the sophisticated socialite who knew precisely what wine to order at dinner to complement their meal. No, she was...sexy as hell right now.

Evie simply nodded at him, as if encouraging him.

He didn't need any encouragement. He simply didn't like the thought of her rushing into danger. And now that he'd realized he knew so little about her past, he also realized she must have rushed into danger who knew how many times before. That knowledge made his skin crawl. She had either been CIA or DIA, he guessed. And his money was on CIA, considering her background. She would have been a great asset to them. Well-educated, spoke multiple languages, attractive. And she knew her way around disguises. That was the clincher for him.

"What do you see on the drone?" he asked Samara, keeping his tone low.

"He's on his phone, still shirtless and pacing around the room."

"Come on, let's move in now. I just want to talk to him," Evie said, as if Dylan would believe that.

He simply shot her a dry look as they approached the outer perimeter of the two-story stucco house that was in desperate need of pressure washing. There were far too many properties in Miami that had gone into foreclosure because of bad banking practices. And this was one of them. At least the trees and shrubs were overgrown, giving them even more cover under the night.

"We go in together," he said quietly as they approached the west side of the house. It was covered in huge bay windows.

She simply nodded as they tested one window, then the next. All the windows were locked so they moved around to the front of the house. Same deal.

On the other side, they found one window that was completely missing a lock on it. Someone had shoved a stick inside, trying to hold it closed, but they managed to wiggle it open.

"How are we looking?" Evie said so quietly he barely heard her.

"You guys are good. He's doing push-ups now." Dylan could practically see Samara rolling her eyes as she said it.

He wasn't sure what he thought of her yet, but it was clear she and Evie cared for each other. His own friend Finn had asked about Samara in a very nonprofessional manner a couple times. Something Dylan was not getting involved in.

"Come on," Evie said quietly.

Even though he knew it annoyed her, Dylan slipped through the window first into what would have once been a bedroom, with hardwood floors and painted gray walls with holes punched in them.

Weapon up, he moved toward the doorway with Evie right behind him.

They both swept out into the hallway. No surprise, empty.

Their shoes made faint sounds on the hardwood as they hurried down the hallway. Since there was no furniture in the place—none that he'd seen anyway—and the ceilings were high, their movements definitely echoed faintly.

Adrenaline pumping, he hurried to the stairs, he and Evie striding up quietly at the same time.

He heard a man talking in low tones.

"He's on the phone again," Samara said through the earpiece. "He looks agitated. He's looking at the doorway. He'll see you if you approach it now."

Evie nodded at him. Making hand gestures as they reached the top of the stairs, she indicated they should enter fast and hard.

He nodded back. The door was open, faint light streaming out into the hallway. More holes had been punched into the walls.

"He's turned away now, but he's still on the phone. Still looks angry." Samara's words were clipped.

Evie held a finger to her lips. Delectable lips he'd kissed far too many times. And wanted to kiss again.

He nodded once.

Weapons up, they swept into the room, but Seamus must have sensed them. The man turned, already starting to draw a weapon from his waistband.

"Drop it or I drop you." Evie's tone was calm, but there was a sharp, deadly edge to it. Something he'd never heard from her before. Not like this. Because there was no doubt in his mind that she meant every word she said to this man.

Seamus looked at her, then Dylan, with a flicker of recognition, before he looked back at Evie. "Nice wig, Bishop."

"Toss your phone over here," Evie commanded.

The man's jaw clenched once but he dropped the phone onto the ground. Then he set the weapon down as well.

"Kick it over to me." A soft, menacing order.

Dylan was silent, letting her run the show as he took a step away from her. He created distance between them in case the guy decided to rush them. Seamus couldn't take them both on if they were spread far enough apart. Simple logistics.

Seamus seemed to realize this as he paused, then kicked the weapon and phone over to her, one at a time.

Evie smashed the phone underneath her foot before kicking the weapon toward one of the walls, far away from all of them.

"What the hell are you doing here, Bishop?" Seamus growled, a vein popping in his neck.

"I ask the questions. Why are you in town?" she demanded.

The man crossed over to the mattress and collapsed on it.

"No way. I know you've got more than one weapon. Stand up," Evie snapped out.

Seamus's jaw tightened as he looked at her then looked at Dylan. "You got anything to say, big guy?"

Dylan simply stared at him. Hard.

Seamus shoved to his feet. As he walked away from the mattress, Dylan approached it and lifted it up. Sure enough there were two pistols underneath it.

"Nice try." Evie's tone was filled with derision. "Why are you in Miami?"

"None of your business. I don't work with you anymore. What I do on my own time is my business."

"Not if your business involves shooting at me."

The guy paused and Dylan thought he saw real surprise flicker in the man's dark eyes. But he didn't know the guy well enough to know.

"What the hell are you talking about?" Seamus said.

"People from a certain op we worked are dead." She flicked a glance at Dylan once and he wasn't sure what crossed her expression in that moment. He couldn't get a read on her right now and he didn't like it. "Xiao and Kalinec are dead. Then someone shot Samara and then shot at me. So either you're gunning for us, or someone is gunning for all of us."

Seamus straightened. "What job?"

Before Evie could answer, Samara said, "Shit! Feds coming in hot right now."

"Repeat that," Evie said.

"I said 'what job'?" Seamus snapped.

Evie touched her ear once. "Not talking to you."

"Team of four moving in hot. They've all got on those stupid blue windbreakers. No IDs but I recognize one of the agents. It's the FBI for sure."

"Get out of there," Evie snapped to Samara.

Dylan looked at Evie, eyebrows raised in a silent question—*What the hell should we do now?*

"You working with the Feds?" she demanded of Seamus.

Seamus simply ran a hand over his face. "Bishop, I seriously want to kick your ass right now," he muttered, but there was no heat in his words, just annoyance.

"They see me!" Samara shouted through the earpiece. "Yep, they're coming for me. Hell." A car door opened. "Hey, watch my ass," she shouted before the line went dead.

"Stay or go?" Dylan asked even as he heard footsteps stomping through the house. It would be tight, but they could try to escape.

Evie motioned for Dylan to go into the attached bathroom. "In there."

"You're out of your mind if you think I'm leaving you alone."

"Just trust me," she snapped. Then she strode toward Seamus and yanked the man in front of her, using him as a shield. "I need to make sure it's really the Feds."

Dylan didn't like what she was doing, but he slipped into the shadows, holding on to his weapon as he moved.

Two seconds later, four people stormed inside through the bedroom door—two men and two women. Dylan was still out of their line of sight. Though if they'd been monitoring the house—and clearly they were—they would have seen him too.

"Don't shoot her," Seamus snapped.

"Evie Bishop," the female voice shouted. "Put that weapon down now. And where's your partner?"

"Ah, hell." Evie shoved Seamus out of the way even as she tossed her weapon onto the bed. Then she looked over at Dylan and nodded. He put his weapon on the floor and kicked it out, coming out of the bathroom with his hands up, mirroring Evie's movements.

From a legal standpoint, he wasn't too concerned about what they'd done. They'd broken into a foreclosed home and he couldn't imagine the bank that owned it would want to prosecute him. Not when he had a huge account there.

A brown-skinned woman with pale gray eyes stepped farther into the room, looking between the two of them. Her jaw clenched tight when it landed on Evie again. "You both have a lot to answer for right now. Hands behind your back!"

"Is this how you saw tonight going?" Dylan asked Evie, doing as the agent ordered.

Evie let out a startled snort-laugh at his question. "Not exactly."

CHAPTER FOURTEEN

"You're going to answer my questions right now," Special Agent Leah Decker said, glaring at Evie from across the table.

They'd been going at this for the last thirty minutes—well, Decker had been, threatening her with all sorts of action. Evie was done listening at this point. She wanted to see Dylan and make sure he was okay. "No, you're going to give me my attorney—the one I requested an hour ago." Evie kept her tone and expression calm as she stared at a woman she'd worked with on more than one occasion. They didn't have much on her and Dylan. Or Samara for that matter.

Yeah, they'd broken into a foreclosed home but...so what? Had they held pistols on Seamus? Yes. But he'd had three weapons as well. It didn't look good, but at this point Evie was almost certain Seamus was working with the Feds. They weren't going to do anything to her or Dylan. If they did, they'd have to admit that Seamus was working for them in the first place. She'd been with the CIA long enough that she understood how things worked and it was pretty clear he was undercover. Or she assumed so. They wouldn't want any of this to become public.

She shifted slightly against the table, the chain on her handcuffs rattling against the cold metal table. "And is this really necessary?" She glanced down at the cuffs.

Before Decker could respond the door opened, and to Evie's surprise Agent Georgina Lewis stepped inside. She looked at Decker, who was also her younger cousin. How she managed to work with Decker all the time, Evie would never know. Even if they were related, Decker was so damn prickly. "Bishop, you're coming with me."

"Are you kidding me?" Decker shoved up from the table. "She almost ruined the cover we've been setting up for months."

And *there* it was. Evie had been wondering what was going on. So Seamus was building up a cover and apparently working with the Feds. If she'd blown his cover, she'd feel remorse—unless he was the person who'd shot at Samara. Then she'd just kick his ass.

Georgina strode to the table and unhooked Evie's cuffs. "Yeah, well, she didn't ruin shit. And you're not going to give her any grief right now. I need to talk to her."

"I swear to God, Georgina—"

"You're not going to do anything, so shut it. She's mine now."

Evie simply blew a kiss at Decker as she walked past the other woman. Yeah, it was super obnoxious but she was in a freaking mood right now. They'd taken both Dylan and Samara, and while she was ninety-five percent sure they were fine, she didn't like being separated from Dylan. If either of them had been hurt, she'd rain down fire on everyone in here. Considering Samara was still healing from a gunshot wound, they'd better have treated her more than just okay.

"Was that really necessary?" Georgina asked as she led her down the hallway of the local FBI office and away from the interrogation rooms.

"No. But I like getting under her skin." Leah had always been such a cranky Girl Scout type, the opposite of Evie.

"Mission accomplished." Georgina sighed as they reached an office door, opened it up. "You're lucky I was here when you guys got brought in."

"So I take it Seamus is *not* a dirty CIA agent?" she asked as they stepped inside Georgina's office.

"Bingo. He's still an agent, but he's working with us. And you almost blew his cover." Her friend's expression turned hard.

Hell. "Did I blow his cover?" Because if he really was working for them, and had nothing to do with the attack on Samara and her, she would find a way to make amends. Even if Seamus was kind of an asshole in general, he was still good at his job. And the Seamus she'd known had been a good agent and cared about bringing down terrorists.

"No. And Leah didn't know it was you at first. The only reason you didn't get shot is because they realized it was Samara out in the SUV."

Evie made a little *hmm* sound and sat in front of Georgina's desk.

"So what the hell are you doing?" Georgina continued. "Why did you come after Seamus?"

Evie was silent for a moment before she ran over the details of what had happened to her and Samara over the past few days. Georgina was a good agent and she trusted her. She'd known the other woman for nearly a decade, and while they didn't often work together, Georgina had put her neck out on the line for victims more than once. For no other reason than it was the right thing to do. And Evie respected her for how willing she was to do what was necessary for the voiceless and powerless.

When she was done, Georgina sat back in her own chair. Gray eyes similar to Leah's were filled with speculation. "That lines up with what Samara told me. And considering she's been shot, I'm going to go out on a limb and say I believe you. But what the hell were you thinking going in there with Samara and a civilian?"

"I was thinking I wanted to get some answers." And Dylan had military experience. "Where was Seamus two nights ago?"

"He's been under surveillance for the last three months. He can't take a shit without Leah's team knowing. He's working a sting operation right now, trying to infiltrate a group, and I can't tell you more than that. What I can tell you is that there is no way he snuck off to shoot the two of you on two separate occasions without being missed. That man has been busy with other things."

Evie inwardly cursed. Georgina had no reason to lie to her. So they were back at square one as far as she and Samara were concerned. Well, maybe not. At least they could mark Seamus off their suspect list. Not much, but Evie would take it. Now they needed to narrow their suspect pool way the hell down.

"Why not reach out to somebody at the Agency if you think your former team is being killed?" her friend asked.

"I did. But I don't think I have all the details right now." She was clearly missing some key piece to all this and she was going to drive herself crazy trying to figure out what.

Georgina sighed, her expression tightening as she sat forward. "Since I've got you here, off the record, we brought someone in for the bombing."

Evie straightened in her chair as well, all thoughts of Seamus fading. The only bombing Georgina could be referring to was the one that had landed Evan in the hospital and killed others. Her heart rate kicked up at the thought of the guilty party being brought to justice. "You're serious?"

"Yeah. It's why I was here tonight. We've been pulling a lot of overtime. I can't say with certainty that he's the guy, but between us…he's the guy, Bishop. We've got him, we just have to nail him to the wall."

Evie wasn't sure whether to be relieved or not. Could they really have caught the guy? She knew Georgina and her team were good. "How sure are you?"

"Again, off the record, it's his signature. And the evidence we have... Let's just say, it's a lot. He had a beef with one of the people killed in the bombing. I can't tell you more than that. I wish I could, but I've got to do this by the book and I won't do anything that risks screwing it up. I'm not letting this guy go. We should be wrapping up this case very soon. Your brother and the others will get justice."

Throat tight, Evie nodded. That was incredible news. She wanted to ask for the bomber's name, but knew Georgina would never give it to her. She couldn't share the news with her family just yet, but knowing that whoever had tried to kill Evan and had killed Isla's dad and others would get what they deserved was a huge relief. Because whoever had set up the bomb had been skilled. They'd known exactly what they were doing when they'd bypassed security.

"Thank you, Georgina. Seriously."

The agent nodded and gave her an appraising look. "By the way, how did you drag that fine-ass man in there with you tonight, anyway? I *know* who Dylan Blackwood is."

Evie lifted a shoulder, half-grinning. "We have a history together and...he wouldn't let me go alone." And she was desperate to see him again, even if she was suppressing her need to get to him. To see with her own eyes that he was okay. "He better be unharmed."

"You know better than that. He's fine." Sighing, Georgina shook her head as she continued. "I can't stay long with you. We've got more interviews and paper-work. You know how it goes."

"So are we being charged with anything?" Evie knew the answer but wanted it crystal clear.

"Hell no. None of this ever happened. There isn't even going to be a record of you three being brought in tonight. And you better not say a word about Seamus—"

"Please! Give me more credit than that." Georgina never would have told her anything at all if she hadn't trusted Evie.

"I might if you hadn't pulled that stunt tonight."

"Like I knew he was undercover. So...he 'left' the Agency under a black cloud. I'm guessing that part was intentional?" Evie wanted to make sure she had all the details straight.

Georgina simply stared at her, not answering one way or another, which was an answer in itself. It probably meant that Seamus's cover involved actually being who he was. They might have faked his firing under the guise of suspecting him of stealing a bunch of money. The CIA had done it before. So Seamus's cover would be as a disgraced, greedy CIA agent. But that wasn't her problem now. And she mentally wished him luck on whatever job he was running.

Evie stood, wanting only to see Dylan, then get Samara. "Pass on my apologies to him?"

"Will do. And I don't want to see you skulking around Miami again."

Evie made a sort of noncommittal sound because she certainly couldn't make that promise.

And now that she knew Seamus wasn't the one gunning for them...that created a new problem. One that meant she would definitely be "skulking" around Miami. She would do whatever was necessary to find out who wanted them dead.

And why.

A ndrew intently listened as the doctor spoke to the security guy at Dylan Blackwood's residence. His heart pounded in his ears as he waited in the trunk, hoping they didn't do a full check of the doctor's vehicle. He'd been watching this place for days and so far they didn't seem to check all vehicles. Not when they knew the people stopping by. It was why he hadn't tried to sneak in using a delivery vehicle because of the thorough checks on those. And an entrance from the water was out—too much room for error.

Andrew had realized the only way he was going to get to Evie Bishop and Samara Sousa—who he now knew was staying here—was by breaking in.

It was risky but the man who'd hired him was willing to pay a lot. And that was what mattered to him. He would take out anyone for the right price. Except kids. He wasn't a total monster.

A second later, the vehicle started forward with a jerk. After less than a minute, the doctor parked and the car went quiet.

He remained as still as possible as he turned on his mic. Earbuds already in, he waited and listened. He heard various guards talking, their voices ebbing and flowing as they walked the perimeter. Blackwood was rich as hell, owning a good portion of the property in

Miami. It was no wonder he had security. His mistake was getting tangled up with Bishop. After that clip on the news of the two of them, the man who'd hired Andrew had sent him here. Said it made sense Bishop would be here. And his boss was convinced that Samara was with Bishop.

After surveying the house from a boat about half a mile out the last couple days, he had their security movements mapped out fairly well. He wanted to stay in the trunk longer, get a better feel for things outside, but wasn't sure how long the doctor was staying.

He waited another twenty minutes until the perfect opening arose. And this was the opportunity he couldn't pass up.

During a lull in the noise, with ski mask in place and gloved hands he silently popped open the trunk. He slipped out and silently shut the trunk, his dark clothes blending in with the shadows. It took him only a few moments to get oriented to where he was—west side of the house near the garage. Perfect. From here he knew exactly how to infiltrate.

He turned on a scrambler he'd created himself, knowing it would make the video feeds go all gray and fuzzy for the next minute. Enough time for him to do what was necessary.

On quiet feet, he hurried toward the multicar garage, stopping at the side door. It had a simple enough security panel so he placed a device on it and let it do its magic. Gone were the days of breaking into places using old-school methods.

He heard two male voices in the distance, growing closer.

He checked his watch. *Come on, come on,* he inwardly ordered.

Click.

He quickly popped the device off the panel and slid inside, locking the door behind him. An Aston Martin, an SUV and an old muscle car sat quietly, leaving one space open. A waste of money as far as he was concerned, but when you were as rich as Blackwood, why not own all these vehicles?

Now would get tricky, as he wasn't familiar with the interior of the house. Not completely. He had the basic layout thanks to the architectural plans he'd stolen. Whereas the breaking in had been child's play for someone like him, this would be a test. Luckily it was three in the morning and most people were asleep now. Obviously someone wasn't, since the doctor had been called, but he was hoping everyone's guard would be lowered this time of night.

Using his mic, he listened. Heard nothing from the kitchen on the other side of the door. After another two minutes of silence, he tried the handle but found it was locked. The door handle was a simple enough lock, however.

Using his old-school lock pick, it took two full minutes. So maybe not so simple after all. But still doable. And he hadn't seen any cameras in the garage so he was still feeling good about this.

Adrenaline pumping as he slipped inside, he quickly scanned the empty kitchen. Moonlight streamed in from a few high windows but the room was empty, as was the attached living room. The pool and Atlantic glittered beyond the windows of the living room, sparkling under the moonlight and city lights.

Instinctively, he adjusted his ski mask as he pulled his SIG out. He didn't like messy jobs, but if he ran up against unexpected resistance, so be it. He was taking out Bishop and Sousa if they were here.

And anyone else who got in his way.

Keeping his earbuds in, he listened outside every room as he moved throughout the house, navigating through the long, winding hallways toward the bedrooms.

When he reached the east wing, he heard multiple voices inside one of the bedrooms. There was also the sound of a shower running and a woman giggling.

Perfect. They might be awake, but they wouldn't be ready for him.

He tried the handle. Unlocked. Even better.

As he stepped into what turned out to be a gigantic bedroom, he saw clothes tossed onto the floor, and rumpled, expensive-looking sheets twisted on a king-size bed.

The door to the attached bathroom was cracked open, steam billowing out.

He heard another very feminine laugh as he approached the door, SIG up.

He wasn't certain if this was Bishop or Sousa. Both were fine pieces of ass. Unfortunately he didn't have time on this op to enjoy either one of them.

No, his priority was to eliminate both of them. For what crime, he had no idea. He just knew they had to die.

He eased the door open but froze at the feel of metal touching the back of his skull.

"Drop it," a deadly male voice said, steel in the words.

He started to turn, then something slammed against the side of his head.

Training kicked in and he twisted, shoving up with his elbow as he turned. Dylan Blackwood dodged the blow, slamming his own fist against Andrew's nose.

Pain exploded in his face as a female voice shouted, "Drop it!"

Evie Bishop stepped out of the shadows of the partially open closet door, fully dressed, pistol raised.

Son of a bitch.

Knowing it was over, he dropped his weapon, resisting the urge to wipe away the blood on his face. He knew Bishop wouldn't outright kill him. No, she would simply call the cops or the Feds. And he wouldn't stay in jail for very long. Hell no. The person who had hired him would make sure he got out immediately. He knew too much, and if anyone killed him, all that information would go public. So he'd take the loss now and live to see another day.

"You're a moron for thinking you could break in here." Blackwood's eyes blazed with anger. "But thank you for putting yourself on camera. Now we have all the evidence the cops will need."

He barely saw the fist coming before Dylan punched him in the face again. This time blackness engulfed him.

CHAPTER SIXTEEN

"Got it," Evie said as she quickly scanned the guy's fingerprints into her mini biometric fingerprint scanner. She didn't start the program to run his info just yet, however. "You know, we could just kill him and ditch the body." She was joking. Mostly. Because she was sick of being targeted. Dylan's security had scanned another heat signature in the trunk of Finn's car—which was how they'd known the man was in there. So security had kept an eye on the vehicle and let the guy think he'd broken in. His tech had been impressive but not good enough.

Finn coming tonight had been by chance—since Samara had contacted him for what Evie was pretty sure was a booty call. Something she wasn't even going to think about. Which told her that Finn had been under surveillance. So whoever was after her and Samara knew Evie was with Blackwood. Probably because of that stupid news clip.

Dylan narrowed his gaze at her as he bound the man's hands behind his back. "I can't tell if you're kidding."

She lifted a shoulder as Dylan secured his feet next. "Carlito is going to get really sick of hearing from us." And she was tired of involving the cops in anything. It went against all her training and instinct in general.

"Probably so."

Evie was silent for a long moment as she stared down at the man. "He looks familiar. I can't figure out where I've seen him though. But there's a good probability that my team has worked with him or hired him. It might come to me before we get a hit on the prints. And if he has worked for my former employer, then...chances are if I run his prints, whoever hired him is going to get wind of it."

"They're going to get wind of it once he gets put into the system," Dylan said.

He'd be charged with a crime, his fingerprints run, and anyone who was keeping tabs on him would know he'd failed in his mission. "Shit," she muttered. "Unless..."

"What?"

"Maybe we don't call the cops. Maybe we call the FBI instead. I know enough people who owe me a favor to hold him for forty-eight hours before having to put him into the system. It's a gamble. But I want to figure out who sent him, before whoever that is realizes he's been arrested."

Dylan was silent for a long moment then nodded. "Okay. Call your contact. I'm going to send Finn home."

"Samara will be sad," she murmured.

Dylan simply snorted and shook his head as he lifted the guy off the ground.

* * *

Less than ten minutes later, Evie stood next to Samara and Dylan as she stared at the computer screen on his desk, reading over Andrew Trent's redacted file. The man Dylan had knocked out in his bedroom was a hired mercenary who did contract work for the CIA. She'd known he'd looked familiar. Trent took any job given to him, no questions asked. A freaking robot as far as she was concerned.

Leo had taken their prisoner and was keeping him secured under his supervision—though he wasn't happy about it and he'd made sure Evie knew it. Not that she blamed the guy. She'd brought nothing but trouble into Dylan's home.

"He's been connected to a lot of operations." She read over what she could, making notes of important things.

Samara's jaw was tight as she reached over and scrolled down, showing the full list of names Trent had worked with, pausing on one in particular. His name had been highlighted more than once and there was an interesting pattern to their communications. Oh...this was not good.

Then Samara looked at Evie, eyebrows raised. "Could it be him?" she murmured.

Evie didn't say anything, simply looked back at the screen as her anger rose. Stepping away from the computer, she pulled out one of her encrypted phones and called a familiar number.

Her longtime friend, and one of her mentors, Luca Ramos answered. "Yeah?"

"It's Evie. Long time no talk. How've you been?" Lead settled in her stomach as she thought about the ramifications of what she was about to do. Her tone sounded light enough, masking the tension building inside her.

"Evie, good to hear your voice. Things are good enough. Working. Wife's still putting up with me, thank God. You know how it is. How's Miami? You settling in? Shit— Sorry, I didn't even think about your brothers," he said almost immediately after asking his first casual questions.

"Yeah, it's been pretty tough. Things have a way of working themselves out." She certainly hoped so anyway. No matter what, she would make sure Ellis never went to jail for a crime he hadn't committed. She would set him up with a new ID if necessary. Get him established in another country with a new life. Whatever it took. He sure as hell wasn't going to jail.

"Isn't that the truth. What do you need from me? You need help with your brother's case? That whole mess stinks of a cover-up. And I hear he's gone off-grid."

Of course Luca had. The man seemed to know everything. Well, maybe not everything. She rubbed at her temple, fighting off a headache. "No, I was just checking in, seeing when you're returning to the States."

"A month, give or take. Working on something big."

"Okay, look me up when you get back. We'll catch up over dinner."

"Sounds like a plan. And let me know if you need help with anything revolving around your family. I'll call in favors. Whatever it takes."

"I will, thanks." Shoving out a breath, she tucked her phone back in her pocket and turned to Samara and Dylan—the man she'd never stopped loving. "It's time to bait a trap."

They both nodded at her. She needed to explain a lot to Dylan, though by now he'd figured out she'd worked for the CIA. Considering the files he'd just looked at, he knew. But she would confirm it for him.

Part of Evie wanted to tell him that he could walk away at any time, that he didn't have to be involved any further than this. But she knew if she did, it would insult him.

The truth was, she didn't want to walk away from him, didn't want him to walk away from her, from what they'd found together. She'd discovered that she *liked* working with him. It was exhilarating in an entirely different way than she was used to. As soon as this was over, she was coming clean, she'd decided. She'd tell him the truth: that she'd targeted him, watched him for a month and then used him as an asset to get an introduction to Rod Jensen.

Then she would let the chips fall where they may. Unfortunately she was pretty sure this was going to end with her heartbreak.

* * *

Five hours later, Evie shoved her laptop away at around the same time Dylan did, and pumped a fist into the air. They'd been going about things all wrong, looking in the wrong corners. After finding out who Andrew Trent had been working with on a regular basis, things made more sense and she'd had a much better idea who was after them.

"What did you find?" Samara asked, rubbing her eyes and yawning.

Evie turned her laptop around at the same time Dylan did. She grinned when she saw one of the same bank accounts she'd found on his laptop screen as well. "Someone has been a very naughty boy," Evie said.

"He's greedy is what he is," Samara muttered.

Yep. Greedy indeed. "Are you ready for this?" Evie asked, looking at her friend.

They'd mostly worked out what they were going to do, how they were going to set the trap for their prey, but it would be tricky to bring down a veteran with the CIA. To bring down someone who had more experience than them. But they had to do it and they had to do this right. For an op like this to work, there was no room for error. Trent had already been picked up by the Feds and she trusted Georgina to keep him under lock and key for now.

And they'd texted the man they were going to bring down from Trent's burner phone, telling him that Evie and Samara weren't at Dylan's house, but that Trent had a bead on where they were and was just trying to narrow it down. All part of laying out the trap.

Samara simply nodded. "I'm ready. He's going down." Then she pulled out an encrypted satellite phone and dialed a number. A few moments later she said, "I know what you did. And you're going to clear out one of your black ops slush funds and put it into my offshore account."

There was a long moment of silence as Samara listened to whatever their target was saying.

Then Samara gave a sharp grin. "I don't care how hard it is to get it. You've done it before—something we both know. And you'll do it again. You tried to have me killed. And now I know what you've done. You will pay me what I want. You've got twelve hours or I'm going public with what I know. I'll send you the account number." Then she hung up.

Evie shoved out a breath. "I hope that's enough."

"That'll be enough," Dylan said. "I believed you at least."

Evie certainly hoped so. Right now they could be making the biggest mistake of their lives. But she would bet that he wouldn't simply pay Samara the money. No, he'd come after her, try to kill her. He likely didn't even believe the blackmail—which was the point of this setup.

"Now it's your turn." Samara handed the phone back to Evie.

Evie simply groaned and sat in the nearest chair next to Dylan's desk.

"Don't be a baby."

"I'm not. Just thinking about the ramifications of all this," Evie said even as she dialed a familiar number.

Georgina picked up on the second ring, sounding exhausted. "Who the hell is this and how do you have my number?"

"It's me. I need a favor."

There was a short pause. "Really, another one? Because I've got one of your 'favors' in holding right now, who I still haven't charged with a crime. And I don't even know why." The federal agent's voice was dry.

Yeah, Evie had called her and asked her to pick Trent up hours ago with the promise that she'd explain everything as soon as she could. That time had come. "I told you I'd explain why. Now I've got something that will get you a big bust. Absolutely huge. You might even get a promotion. But you're not going to like it."

"You're killing me, Bishop. But I'm listening."

CHAPTER SEVENTEEN

"He's on a plane." Evie ended the call as she set her cell phone on the dresser of the bedroom she would be staying in tonight. Not Dylan's bed, and not in his house, unfortunately. But that couldn't be helped. Their prey was going to come to them, no doubt. She knew he wouldn't give in to blackmail and right now he probably assumed he had the upper hand.

Dylan looked out the window onto the quiet street. "I don't like any of this."

"He's coming to Miami. That's a good thing." Setting up a sting operation here made the logistics of everything a lot easier than if they'd had to go to him. Luckily the traitor had made things easy on them.

Dylan shoved away from the window and moved toward her in long, angry strides. "I know. But he's got to know this is a trap."

"Yes. That's kind of the whole point."

His jaw tightened, that familiar look of frustration firmly in place. "The backup team will be too far away."

She placed her hands on his chest. "He's a pro. If they're too close, he'll know and this opportunity will be lost. We need to bring him down. I have a feeling this goes deeper than just stolen money." Obviously, considering that he'd tried to have Samara and Evie

179

killed. She still didn't know why, not exactly, but she would get those answers.

Dylan rested his hands on her hips, pulling her close, his dark green eyes flashing with too many emotions. "Let me stay here, then."

She ran her fingers up his chest, savoring the feel of his muscles underneath her fingertips before she clasped them behind his neck. "We've been over this," she whispered.

"I don't care." His jaw was tight.

"You might be king of the world and fully capable of taking part in this op, but you are still a civilian. You can't stay." The FBI would never allow it. They would let him stay with them at the command center blocks away, but not here at the house. It was an impossibility. "Besides, he's going to do a sweep of the house. If he sees more than two heat signatures, he'll suspect something."

Dylan frowned so she leaned up on tiptoe and kissed him hard.

He didn't resist, his tongue tangling with hers as he backed her up to the closest wall. Samara was downstairs with their small team, getting ready for what was to come. Evie didn't care about any of that. She simply needed this moment with Dylan.

Reaching out, she fumbled around until she turned the flimsy lock on the door. She didn't care if everyone downstairs figured out what they were doing. She loved Dylan and she wanted him safe. She wanted this whole thing over so they could have a future—if he managed to forgive her.

Dylan would have to leave soon and she was going to wring every moment of pleasure out of the here and now. Because at the end of the day, she knew she might not survive this. That was always a chance on operations, that things would go sideways, and now was no different. Especially since they were toeing a very fine line with how they'd baited this trap. She was on a razor's edge, hoping she didn't fall. Because this time, no matter how capable he was, Dylan couldn't catch her.

Dylan slid his hand through her hair, cupping the back of her head, kissing her hard enough to leave her lips swollen.

When he tore his mouth away, his expression was savage. "I can just kill him," he growled. "Be done with this whole thing."

She blinked, staring at him because…she believed him. "You don't mean that."

"Don't I? If he was dead, you'd be out of danger." Pure, raw truth was in his voice.

She shuddered at his words, his protectiveness. It shouldn't turn her on, but it did. "We can't do that. Even if I want to take him out myself. We need to find out how deep his betrayal goes. Right now isn't just about my safety. It's about the safety of our country. He could be selling secrets. Hell, he probably *is.* There's a reason he went after Samara and then me. He's into something bad and we need to know everything. We

182 | KATIE REUS

need to know where he's funneling his money." Once
that happened, everything else would unravel.

That was why her very first team leader had always
told her to "follow the money." They'd found some of
their target's accounts but it wasn't enough. They
needed more.

By his expression, she knew Dylan didn't like what
she was saying but he also didn't argue with her. Instead, he kissed her again.

She let herself fall into the kiss and into his embrace
as he reached for the hem of her shirt. She needed all of
him right now. This was more than about wanting a
simple connection; she was desperate for Dylan's touch,
his kisses.

Greedily, she reached for the buckle of his pants,
shoving at his clothing as he shoved at hers.

She felt manic, frenzied. With him it had always
been too much and never enough. Dear God, it was
never enough. He had a hold on her and had from the
moment they'd met. It hadn't mattered that she'd been
undercover. She hadn't been acting with him. Not
about her feelings. She'd never even intended to sleep
with him, just get him to take her out on a few dates
and make introductions. But it was like he'd reached inside her soul and seen the real her.

He went down on his knees as he yanked off her
pants, completely undressing her. Then he grabbed her
calf and threw her leg over his shoulder.

"Dylan." She barely got his name out before his
mouth was between her legs, teasing her slick folds.

She arched off the wall, rolling her hips against his face. His tongue was wicked and perfect. So very perfect.

Her nipples tightened even as her clit pulsed, needing more pressure. She felt as if all her nerve endings were tightened in awareness as he flicked his tongue along her folds. Teased and tortured.

She slid her fingers through his hair, wondering how she would live without him if he couldn't forgive her. She had to tell him the truth and she would. As soon as this operation was over. For now, she would enjoy every second of this, memorize every moment and hold on to him for as long as she could.

She needed to have her head on straight, and if he rejected her later, her mind would be all haywire. No, she would tell him tomorrow. Or hell, later tonight. However long it took to get this thing done.

"You are so wet," he rasped out.

"Always, for you." She could barely get the words out as he slid a finger inside her. The man drove her absolutely crazy with need.

He added another finger and began stroking, sliding them in and out of her as he focused on her clit.

There it was. His tongue was the perfect pressure. "Hell," she groaned.

"Say my name," he growled against her sensitive bundle of nerves, sending a vibration of pleasure through her.

He was always so damn demanding and she found it incredibly sexy. "Dylan," she moaned, keeping her voice as low as she could. Screw it if anyone could hear them. She needed this and so did he.

Anything could happen in the next few hours.

He increased his pressure on her clit, driving her insane as he buried another finger inside her. That sent her completely over the edge, her orgasm peaking so sharp and fast she hadn't been ready for it.

As he stood up, she practically jumped him, wrapping her arms around him as he shoved her up against the wall. She arched into him, her breasts rubbing against his chest as he grabbed the backs of her thighs and hoisted her up.

Positioning himself, he drove deep inside her, a groan tearing from his throat. Her inner walls tightened around him as he began thrusting inside her.

She felt filled by him in more ways than one. Unexpected tears sprang to her eyes as he thrust over and over, harder and harder. Like if he fucked her hard enough, he could infuse himself into her body and heart so that when he left, she would still know he was with her. She didn't want to let him go tonight, but she had to.

The outcome of tonight mattered. Dylan mattered too, more than anyone or anything. But this had to be done.

She kissed him, nipping his bottom lip as he cupped one of her breasts. His thrusts were hard but his caresses gentle, the contradiction making all the muscles in her body pull taut.

Everything he did was absolute perfection. She could barely wrap her head around this connection between them, this fire and heat that spread everywhere.

When he reached between their bodies and tweaked her clit again, little tremors started deep inside her. That first climax had barely taken the edge off. She hadn't thought she'd be able to get off a second time, but she was already beginning the climb as he continued thrusting.

"Come," he demanded.

Everything with him was always a demand.

And her body wanted to obey, wanted to give him exactly what he demanded. Her orgasm slammed through her, this one sharper than before. In that moment he let himself go, coming inside her, groaning her name as he buried his face against her neck.

She felt their wetness against her inner thighs as he held her in place, pinning her to the wall. She wasn't sure how long they stayed like that, breathing hard, wrapped up in each other. It didn't matter. She didn't want this to end yet. Didn't want to pull away.

Finally he unwound her legs and gently set her on the floor. Her knees were weak as he continued kissing her, pushing her back up against the wall as he dominated her mouth.

She sank into it, clutching him in desperation. She didn't want to wipe his scent away from her, didn't want to step away from him to clean up, didn't want to leave him at all. Because deep down she was terrified this might be the last time they would ever be together.

Because even if she survived tonight, she didn't know if she would survive the heartbreak of Dylan's rejection. She just had to hold on to the hope that he would find it in his heart to forgive her for what she'd done.

To understand why she'd done what she'd done.

And to give her a second chance.

CHAPTER EIGHTEEN

Six months ago

*D*ylan smiled at Evie as she stepped out onto the patio. He'd had the most expensive caterer in town set up everything. He'd known she wouldn't want any type of public spectacle and he didn't like his life on display, regardless. They were very much alike that way, he'd come to realize. She valued her privacy as much as he did. Unlike some of the women he'd dated in the past who had relished being in the gossip section, linked to him and his money, Evie was a private woman who came from money. He knew she wasn't after his, which was something he usually had to worry about. And she hated the spotlight.

She gave him a confused look as she glanced at the spread of gourmet cheeses, fruit, crackers and mini desserts. A bottle of champagne was chilling in the bucket and there were two glasses on the table.

He knew without a doubt this was the woman he wanted to spend the rest of his life with—and he wanted to spend the rest of their lives peeling back all of her complex layers, getting to know everything about her. Evie Bishop was a one-of-a-kind woman.

"You look beautiful," he said, pulling her into his arms.

"You don't look so bad yourself," she said, confusion still lingering in her eyes. But she leaned up on tiptoe and brushed her lips over his.

"Evie, there's something I want to ask you." His heart was racing as he went down on one knee and pulled the jewelry box out of his pocket. *Normally he knew what the outcome of something would be, and while he was almost positive she would say yes, doubt still lingered in the back of his mind. She kept him on his toes, kept him guessing what would come out of her mouth all the time. And he wanted to lock her down, to make it clear to everyone that she was taken.*

Evie's eyes widened, her face paling. "No," *she whispered, her expression stricken.*

He frowned. "Evie?"

She was shaking her head as she tugged him to his feet. "No, Dylan. Please, no."

His gut twisted as if she'd physically punched him—with a sledgehammer.

"No, don't propose to you?"

Tears glistened in her eyes as she shook her head. "I didn't know... I can't do this. I'm sorry. I'm so sorry." *It was the first time he'd seen her cry since they'd met. The raw anguish on her face confused him.*

He tried to push away the hurt her rejection caused. "Why not?"

"Dylan, we've been having so much fun. The last six months have been incredible. But... We can't get married."

Feeling numb, he shoved the ring back in his pocket. "We can't?"

"I..." *She looked around the patio, glancing up at the sparkling twinkle lights he had set up for tonight. She looked sick as she stared at everything, her expression full of horror.*

Horror, really? How could he have read her so wrong? How could he have read the situation so badly? He was ready to take the next step with her, wanted to have a full, long life with Evie.

"It's not you, it's me," *she blurted, making this so much worse.*

For the first time in his life, he wasn't sure what the hell to do. How to react. He sat in one of the nearest chairs at the table, at a total loss. "How can this surprise you? You had to know we were building to this."

"I'm sorry. I'm moving back to DC soon. This...this would never work." She turned and fled back inside.

He wanted to go after her, to demand answers. But what the hell was he going to do? Ask her why she wouldn't marry him? The reason didn't matter. Clearly she didn't feel the same way he did.

Gutted, he reached out and opened the champagne bottle, the pop of the cork overly loud. He'd planned to open it after she said yes, to celebrate the beginning of their life together. He registered the foam spilling over his fingers but didn't move to clean it up. Completely out of character, he took a swig straight from the bottle. What the hell had just happened?

He was vaguely aware of Leo stepping outside, looking at him with surprise and then pity.

The pity was too much.

"She's gone," Leo murmured. "Left in her car."

Throat tight, he shoved to his feet, not looking at his head of security—his friend. "Make sure someone cleans this up. I don't want to see it." Bottle still in hand, he stalked back inside. Some small part of him hoped that maybe Evie would still be there. But he wasn't sure why. He had nothing more to say to her right now.

Seeing her would just shove the knife deeper in his chest.

He didn't understand what had just happened. He knew she cared for him, thought she'd loved him as much as he loved her. Clearly that wasn't enough. And he didn't understand why.

He took another swig as he headed for his room, hoping the champagne would take the edge off. Take away the pain, if only temporarily.

But he knew it wouldn't. Nothing would. Not when the woman he loved had just run out of his life.

CHAPTER NINETEEN

As he landed at the private Miami airport, his adrenaline spiked. He was here. Soon he would take care of business. Trent had texted him that he had a bead on Samara and Evie. Trent had also told him that he was going dark so he had no way to get a hold of his guy, to tell him he was in town. It didn't matter because he knew where Samara and Evie were.

There was no way Samara was not working with Evie Bishop. Of course they were working together and would no doubt try to set him up. Even though Samara had always been a bit of a wild card, Evie bled red, white and blue. And Samara had gone to her for help. So even if Samara wanted to play him, to demand money...he didn't buy it. Her mistake had been in giving him twelve hours. He was going to use that time to hunt her down and kill her. Bishop too, since they'd likely be together.

He would simply take care of them and then return to life as normal.

There was no way they knew what he'd been involved in. If they did, he would be arrested as a traitor. No, they simply suspected and were trying to set him up. Had to be it.

As he descended onto the tarmac, he nodded once at the pilot he'd asked for a favor. He wasn't using any

Agency resources right now. He was using assets and personal favors for this trip. No one else knew he was in Miami. Not even his wife.

And he would keep it that way. The flight here hadn't taken long and the flight home wouldn't take long either.

He simply needed to clean up this mess before he got caught in it.

The private car he'd rented under an inactive agent's alias was waiting for him. He gave the driver the address as he pulled out his tablet and started working.

It had taken some digging, but finally, *finally*, he'd found out where Samara was staying. He'd thought she'd been at Dylan Blackwood's house since it was clear that Bishop had hooked up with the man again. So when Trent said he had a bead on them, he'd started thinking outside the box.

And he'd gotten lucky. Samara was staying at a two-story house she'd rented through one of those online places where people rented out their homes. She hadn't gotten it under her real name, of course. She'd done exactly what he had, used an inactive agent's credentials as opposed to one of her aliases.

They thought they could come after him? He nearly snarled at the thought. He was smarter than both of them, and soon they would both realize just how deadly he was. They'd never viewed him as a threat. He'd always played his role well, had always been good at the job. But he didn't get paid enough for the threats and danger he dealt with—for the lifestyle he deserved. He wasn't going to one day retire with a pathetic pension and nothing to show for his career. He deserved more.

Once he was through with them, he'd need to dispose of their bodies where no one would ever find them. Luckily they were in Florida so it would be easy enough to take them out to the wetlands and dump them.

Without their bodies, it would be hard to make a case against anyone for their murders. Which was what he was counting on.

* * *

Hours later Evie lay in one of the four bedrooms in the cheerily decorated two-story house. She hated the waiting. Especially since it was in relative silence.

A few dogs barked in the distance. She'd heard a couple car horn blasts earlier and the sound of a boat engine revving by someone who'd decided to go late-night fishing. Or just joy-riding on the lake. Between the random sounds and her thoughts, her thoughts were winning.

She should be focusing on what was to come, on that damn traitor. Instead, she was staring at the ceiling, gearing up to tell Dylan the truth. She had it all planned out in her mind. But every time she imagined it, he walked away when she was done. Because that was the only outcome. Him leaving. *Ugh.*

"I've got movement," Georgina said quietly through her earpiece.

Even though they were on a private frequency, they would be communicating only when necessary. The man they were going to take down was trained so they were being careful.

He would come in here, looking to take out Samara and possibly Evie. They just hoped he didn't see this *particular* plan coming into play.

Neither Evie nor Samara answered, not wanting to give away anything audible. No one had tapped into the comm line, but the traitor could be using a parabolic mic, listening to the house. She and Samara were ready, regardless. This needed to end tonight. Knowing that Dylan was with Georgina in the command center made this easier. She hated that he was worried about her now, but she still liked that he was on the periphery of things.

Rolling over, she snagged her tablet from the bedside table and pulled up the various video feeds from the hidden cameras they had set up outside.

There was a flutter of movement across the street on one feed. The residential neighborhood was quiet, but a shadow peeled off from the side of a house across the street. It had to be him. Unless someone else was lurking about at three in the morning.

No doubt he'd done recon of the place and set up audio listening devices to scan for any chatter. It was what she would do. He would also likely—

Yep, there went the video feeds. He must have sent out a pulse to disable all security cameras in the nearby area.

Easing back, she tucked the tablet into the drawer. Cameras outside were down. But he wasn't as smart as he thought. Once the pulse went out, disabling the current devices, she turned on another set of cameras and started recording.

She withdrew her weapon from under the pillow and moved toward the closet. It was game on.

This traitor was going down.

CHAPTER TWENTY

After setting off the pulse device, he was certain that all cameras Samara might have set up had been disabled. The two heat signatures were in the upstairs bedrooms so he made his entry at the back of the house, where it was dark. Then he activated the electronic jammer before quickly and quietly cutting a hole in one of the downstairs windows.

At this point, they likely suspected something was going on. That was okay, let them suspect. He would still kill Samara and Evie. With his ski mask on, he slipped into what turned out to be a living room.

He was silent as he pulled his NVGs down and his weapon out. Both women were trained but so was he.

His feet were silent as he hurried up the stairs, his rage fueling him to do this. By the time he made it to the top landing, his adrenaline was pumping hard. From his earlier recon, he knew that the first door on the right had someone inside it. And he didn't care who he shot first.

The door was already cracked open so he gently eased it farther open with his foot. Light from outside streamed in through the window across the room but he immediately saw the lump in the bed.

Aiming his weapon, he fired at the bed, the suppressed rounds quiet.

But a figure suddenly stepped out from the closet.

He swiveled and ducked on instinct.

Bullets exploded into the doorframe next to him, barely missing.

He fired center mass at the figure near the closet. Once, twice, the shots muted from his suppressor.

The person dropped with a grunt. He started to step forward, but froze as he heard a wisp of air moving behind him.

Before he could turn, he felt the cold steel of a pistol against his lower spine.

"I would say it's good to see you again, but we both know that's a lie," Samara's steely voice whispered in his ear.

Then she reached around him and shot the still figure by the closet in the head. Then suddenly the room flooded with light.

He shoved his NVGs up. Blinking, he saw Evie lying on the ground with a bullet wound straight through her skull. *Holy hell.* Shock punched through him, but... No...it couldn't be real. He'd seen staged crime scenes before. This had to be fake.

Samara pressed the gun against his back, dug in hard. "You saved me the trouble of doing it myself. Not all of us have rich daddies to take care of them." There was a wealth of bitterness in her voice.

"She's not dead." No way. This was a setup. Even as he stared at Evie's still body, at her unmoving chest...he couldn't believe it.

Samara snorted as she ripped his ski mask off and shoved him forward. "Test her pulse, asshole. But keep your hands in the air as you move."

He did as she ordered, bending down and... *Holy shit.* Bishop was dead. This...wasn't what he had expected. Samara hadn't shot him yet, so she needed him alive at least. Still, unease slid down his spine. "Why'd you do this?"

"I'm doing the talking right now. Keep your hands up and turn around slowly. You and I are about to do some business together, Ben."

A minute later Ben sat down at the kitchen table in the beach-themed kitchen, staring at Samara in surprise. He'd come here expecting a setup—he'd thought Samara and Evie would try to get him to confess to killing Xiao and taking payoffs. He hadn't expected *this.*

Samara had always been the smartass of the team, but he knew that underneath she was an ice-cold operator. She'd been dumped into the foster system at the age of twelve after surviving a horrific childhood. But she'd cleared all her psych tests and she had an aptitude for languages, like Bishop had. Even though she'd never been as polished as Bishop, not in the sort of way that you were when born into wealth, she was a chameleon. Adaptable to situations in a way her upbringing had given her.

"I can't believe you killed her," he said, feeling like a parrot even as fear cut through him. He had to figure out a way to get out of this. He was smarter than this bitch.

Samara lifted a shoulder, her expression neutral. "I didn't want to. And it's not personal. But she wanted to turn you in. Thank you for disabling the cameras, by the way. I knew you would."

He'd thought Samara might expect him, he just hadn't thought she'd be so damn prepared. He'd left DC almost immediately after her call, barely giving her any time to prep for his arrival.

"You never should have sent that hitter after me," she snapped.

He wanted to ask about Trent, but held off. He had to play this right, to see if this truly was a setup. If it was, the Feds would storm the place if he admitted anything. "How'd you get Evie involved?"

She gave him a dry look. "I went to her when your guy shot me. I didn't know it was you at the time, but I finally figured it out. You're not as careful as you think."

He narrowed his gaze, not confirming anything. He wanted to ask how she'd known he'd sent Trent, but if he did, it would be admitting he'd sent someone after her. He might have disabled the cameras and sent out a pulse to neutralize electronics inside the house, but he had to be careful.

"Who'd you send after me?" she asked.

He didn't respond. He still wasn't convinced this wasn't a setup, even with Bishop dead.

Samara tapped her weapon against the kitchen table.

"If you're going to shoot me, just shoot me." Adrenaline mixed with fear settled in his gut as he pushed her.

"Fine. Whoever he is, you're going to call off your dog. And you're going to transfer me two million dollars," she said as she turned a laptop around on the table with one hand.

He shifted slightly, masking his surprise. He'd assumed she would try to get him to confess to something, to trap him. "You think I have two million dollars?"

She snorted. "I know you do. I found some of your accounts. But you don't have to admit to it. Now, you're going to transfer money to me from a couple of your secret black ops slush funds. I know you have access to them and no one will question you."

He'd seen her finances, and while they weren't horrible, she wasn't flush in the way that Bishop was—had been.

Sweat beaded against his upper lip, but he didn't move. He needed to stall. Once she had her money, she'd have no reason to let him live. "You really going to be able to live with killing Bishop?"

She paused, rubbed a hand over the back of her neck, looking only slightly agitated, but she didn't lower her weapon. "I'll live with it. Are you going to be able to live with killing Xiao and Kalinec?"

"They weren't murdered." Well, Samuel Xiao had been. Ben had made it look like a heart attack.

She started again. "Please. I don't believe in coincidence."

"It *was* a coincidence."

She watched him for a long moment.

He lifted a shoulder. "Much stranger things have happened."

"Fine. Now do it." She motioned to the laptop. "It's already set up for you."

"You could kill me anyway."

She smiled at him, a tiger watching its prey. That was when he realized people had always underestimated her. She joked around a lot, but watching her now was like watching a lethal predator. He knew she'd killed, more than once. But she had never seemed to relish it. Now, however, if she really had killed Bishop...

"People underestimate you," he murmured.

"Quit stalling." She shoved the laptop across the table. "Transfer the money to the account number taped at the top of the laptop."

"Why should I?"

She tapped the gun against the table again. "If you don't, I'll kill you. And it won't be an easy death."

"Why don't we work together?" he asked, not moving his hands. Tingles of panic had started to form at the base of his spine as he read the intent in her eyes. She would definitely kill him. He needed to get close enough to disarm her, to take her weapon. He might be a tech geek, but he was damn good in hand-to-hand combat. "Two million isn't much."

She snorted. "Sure it is."

"Not for long. And I thought you were smart. Why not play the long game? I can get you more than just two million."

Her eyes glinted with interest. "Fine, you want to give me money? Add another two to it."

"That's not what I'm talking about. I'm talking about something else."

She watched him closely, her expression tightening. "Quit stalling and transfer the money."

Though he hated to do it, his fingers flew across the keyboard as she came to stand behind him. He could see her in the reflection, see the weapon pointed at the back of his head. "There," he said, hitting the final button. "You've got your money."

"Thank you. Now you're going to take the fall for killing Evie," she said as she leaned forward and closed her computer. Now was the time. He had to take her out.

"What the hell are you talking about?"

"I started putting things together and realized that you were going after people from the Jensen op—"

He lunged at her, tackling her to the ground. She tried to knee him in the groin but he was more skilled in hand-to-hand combat. Her gun clattered across the floor, out of reach. He elbowed her across the face as he yanked his own weapon back. Breathing hard, he held it on her. She lay on the ground, her nose bleeding as she glared up at him.

She was breathing hard now. "You gonna kill me now? Like you killed Kalinec and—"

"Shut the hell up with that. I told you I didn't kill Kalinec. That truly was unfortunate." He waited, wondering if backup would arrive. Up until this point he'd confessed to nothing and he'd transferred money to her under duress. Yeah, he'd shot Evie, but so had she. He could still spin this.

"Lies!" she spat at him.

"I'm not lying. Kalinec getting killed in a mugging was a coincidence." He grabbed the laptop from the table. It was time to go.

Slowly she pushed up from the floor, keeping her hands out at her side as he trained his weapon on her. She stared at him for a long moment. "You're serious. Their deaths so close together really was a coincidence."

He simply smiled at her, enjoying her confusion.

"But you sent someone after me."

Yep. She'd gotten nosy, digging around in his business. Making a heart attack look real was child's play for him. He'd been with the CIA for decades. He wished she'd just left well enough alone. But he wasn't going to waste time explaining to her what he'd done.

"Did you kill Xiao?" she pressed.

Ben motioned for her to back up to the exit. He was going to have to kill her, but it would be easier to do it in the garage and then transfer her body to the car from there. Then he'd have to haul Bishop's body downstairs too, and dispose of them together. Then this house was going to have an accidental fire because he wasn't going to waste time cleaning up the blood. He'd never get it all unless he called in a professional cleaner and he wasn't involving anyone else in this. "Come on, in the garage. Now!"

"How much money are you moving?" Desperation filled her voice as she tried to stall.

"Move or I shoot you here." He wasn't going to spill all his secrets.

"So you're gonna kill me and what?" she finally asked as they entered the garage.

"Then I'm going to dump your body so no one will ever find it."

Fear etched her face as he shut the door behind them. He kept his weapon up. "Turn around."

"Fuck you." She remained where she was.

"Fine." He pulled the trigger.

Ben blinked. Nothing happened. What the hell?

Samara grinned at him, all fear gone. "You're gonna want to get on the ground."

"What?"

"Do it. Hands above your head."

Before he could ask what the hell she was talking about, two armed FBI agents kicked the door in, weapons up.

"Benjamin Miller, you're under arrest for the murder of Samuel Xiao, the attempted murder of Samara Sousa, and for selling state secrets," a female agent he recognized snapped at him as he dropped the useless weapon. "And that's just the beginning." Samara had clearly done something to it—probably removed the firing pin—and like a fool, he'd fallen into her trap. "Hands behind your back."

Even as he complied, he sneered at the FBI agent. "I was under duress. You'll never make anything stick."

Fear punched through him, but he reminded himself that he hadn't admitted to anything.

"You weren't under duress when you pointed a weapon and tried to fire it at your colleague. And thanks to that transfer we've got enough details from you because we've been monitoring that particular account you transferred from. We know where you've been moving your money—and who has been paying you off. And Samara got us curious enough to look into Samuel Xiao's death—he was poisoned and it was made to look like a heart attack. My money's on you killing him. Currently we're digging deep into all of his online activities. If he had anything on you, we'll find it. We have enough to bury you right now."

His gut tightened as her words sank in, as reality started to push in on him, making it hard to breathe. He'd covered his tracks where Xiao had been concerned but...the man had been looking into Ben. It was why he'd killed him in the first place. Not because of the Jensen op. If the Feds found any of Xiao's records... He was screwed.

At that moment, Bishop strode into the room, face freshly washed and hair pulled back in a ponytail.

No. No, no, no. He should have known better. It was incredibly difficult to mask a pulse, but he knew it was possible.

God dammit. When no backup had shown up for Samara he'd fallen for this trap. Now he was screwed.

Even as the agent in charge started dragging him out, Dylan Blackwood strode into the garage, his expression worried.

Ben jerked back in surprise that the man was here at all. Then he looked at Evie, that nosy, self-righteous bitch. He couldn't kill her now, but he could still do damage.

"Did you tell Blackwood that he was your asset? That you set him up a year ago?" he asked, looking at the rich bastard once before glaring at Bishop. From the expression on her face, he knew she hadn't. "Did Evie ever tell you how she targeted you?" he shouted to Blackwood as the agent told him to shut up, dragging him away.

But Ben didn't care. He was going down no matter what, and he was going to hurt Bishop as much as possible.

"Did she tell you how we watched you for a month before that cocktail party at your parents' house? Ask her how she fucked you to get that introduction to Rod Jensen!" He jerked in pain as the agent twisted his arm back even harder, but it was worth it.

"You have the right to remain silent and I suggest you shut the hell up," she growled as she shoved him through the door.

CHAPTER TWENTY-ONE

Evie met Dylan's sharp gaze across the garage, her heart in her throat. Everything around them faded away as she hurried toward him, ignoring the agents in the room. Her part with this op was done. Hell, Dylan shouldn't even be in here, but he must have disobeyed Georgina and left the command center.

He stared at her a long moment, his eyes icy as she reached him. Before he could say anything she grabbed him by the forearm and dragged him inside and into the quiet living room.

"You targeted me?" His voice was deathly quiet.

She wanted to deny it, but nodded. "Yes." He stared at her as if he was staring at a stranger. Which was fair. The hurt and pain in his eyes clawed at her insides. "I wanted to tell you the truth."

"You watched me? Had me under surveillance? Before we met at the party."

Feeling miserable, she nodded. "Yes. I didn't sleep with you as part of the op though. I swear!" Even that sounded bad. God, her stomach was churning, her heart pounding.

He snorted at her declaration. "You swear? I'm not sure how much that matters, considering what your word is worth."

She swallowed hard. "I needed an introduction to Rod Jensen. But my feelings for you were—and are—real."

He blinked in confusion, though the rage still simmered beneath the surface. "Jensen? The man who was killed in prison?"

She nodded. "Yes. You moved in the same circles even though you weren't friends with him. Getting an introduction to him organically was the smartest move for the operation. It's why I was in Miami—I was undercover as myself. But I never meant to hurt you. I never meant to fall for you at all, but I did." She desperately needed him to believe that. "I'm so sorry I lied to you."

He took a step back and on instinct she reached out, grabbing his forearm again. He didn't pull away, just looked at her with too many emotions flickering across his expression. Anger being the foremost. "I don't know what to say to you right now."

"I know it's too much to ask for your forgiveness, but I really am sorry."

"Sorry?" he scoffed. "I proposed to you. I *loved* you. Was this some kind of sick game—"

"No! I told you. After you got me the introduction to Jensen, I should have ended things with you but I couldn't walk away. I couldn't walk away from you. And I know that's selfish on my part. I fell for you," she whispered.

Finally he jerked his arm away and turned from her without a word. His departing icy look was more than enough.

Her chest tightened, her heart breaking as the man she loved strode out the door without a backward glance.

She wasn't sure how long she stood there but when Samara took her arm gently and said, "It's time to go" she didn't fight her.

Evie knew she would need to fill out paperwork and deal with the aftereffects of the op, but Samara simply drove her to her brother's house. She barely remembered getting in bed, but she did and finally let the tears fall.

She had no idea if her friend stayed or left and she didn't care. She just wanted to be alone in her misery. She cried herself to sleep, and when the sun rose, she cried in the shower. Then she cried as she got back into bed and slept some more.

She slept until a familiar ringtone sounded on her phone. Though she wanted to ignore it, she was worried about her brother. "Hey, Mom." Damn it, her voice broke on the last word. The op had been a huge success, but she'd never been so miserable. Without Dylan, her world had no color in it.

"What's wrong, honey?"

"Everything." The floodgates broke again and she couldn't find it in herself to care. She wasn't a crier by nature, but her world had just been shattered and she had only herself to blame. She wanted to grovel, to fight for him, but…she'd seen that look in his eyes. He was done with her.

There was no coming back from this.

* * *

"You look like hell," Georgina said to Evie as she opened her office door, letting both Evie and Samara inside. Everything on her desk was in perfect order, all her files and even her stapler was at a perfect angle.

"Thanks a lot," she muttered. She'd tried calling Dylan half a dozen times, but he hadn't answered. No surprise. She'd been a pathetic mess, barely getting out of bed except to go to the hospital to see her brother. Even though she knew she deserved it, the ache in her chest only grew at her loss.

Georgina simply shrugged and rounded her desk to sit, motioning for them to do the same. "I just wanted to give you an update in person, so thanks for coming down. We've got a whole lot of intel we're sifting through right now. And the CIA is pissed that they weren't brought in on this."

"Yeah, I know," Samara muttered. "I've been in DC the past two days getting reamed out for not bringing them in."

Evie had gotten a call from her former boss, but she'd ignored him. She didn't work for the CIA anymore. "So what's the deal?"

"Turns out that Ben has been selling secrets. Mostly small stuff, but enough to screw up operations and keep the money flowing. And every now and then he gave critical op intel to the wrong parties—and a few of your agents were killed because of it."

Evie bit back a curse. Ben would get what was coming to him. Or he'd better.

"We've processed Andrew Trent and he's been very cooperative with us. He'll do a lot of time, but we've taken the death penalty off the table. He's giving us everything he has on Ben—who's a much bigger threat to national security. It looks as if he injected Xiao with poison and made it look like a heart attack. Everything he admitted to you," she said, looking at Samara, "appears legit. He really did send Trent after you because he thought you'd end up being a problem down the road. Which in hindsight was a mistake, since it only solidified to you that the Jensen job was the link between the two deaths."

"Holy shit," Samara muttered. "So my nosiness is basically what got Ben to come after me?"

"Yep. And it's a good thing too, because he's been flying under the radar for a long time. He's a real piece of work."

"What about Kalinec?" Evie asked.

"As far as we can tell, Ben had nothing to do with it."

"What's going to happen to him?"

"Not sure yet. But I'm betting on the death penalty. He won't see the outside of the cell no matter what. He committed treason. Likely he'll end up in solitary for the rest of his life. However long that may be."

"Luca is safe?" she asked.

Georgina nodded. "Yes. I've spoken to him person-ally. He said if he could be here, he would. He's just as angry as we are that Ben betrayed...everyone."

Evie digested Georgina's words, fighting a wave of exhaustion. She'd called Luca to make sure he was safe and out of the country before they went after Ben. Even though she'd wanted to tell him what they were doing, she'd had to play things close to the vest. She hadn't wanted to risk Ben somehow discovering what they were up to. "Do you need anything else from us?"

Georgina shook her head, then looked at Samara. "Mind stepping out so I can have a word with Evie alone?"

"I'll be in the break room," Samara said to Evie.

"What's up?" Evie asked as the door shut behind her friend.

"First, thank you for what you did. You took a huge risk in that op. I didn't get to tell you that night." Georgina's expression was serious.

Evie shrugged, feeling uncomfortable with the praise. "I had on a vest and a ballistics face mask. It was a small risk." The vest had been high-tech and one of her custom-made pieces, almost impossible to feel be-neath her clothes. Wearing the ballistics mask had been a risk, but on the chance that Ben had tried to take a head shot, she'd had to wear it. When Samara had flipped on the lights, temporarily blinding him, she'd ripped it off and tossed it under the bed. Everything had been choreographed down to the last detail. Even Samara's fake shot to her head. Covering her pulse had been more difficult, but Ben had been jacked up on adrenaline, not paying attention to all his surroundings.

She snorted. "It wasn't small. Anyway, I also wanted to let you know that we've officially booked the bomber. The news will be breaking tonight. I thought you deserved to know ahead of time. He's admitted to his crimes in lieu of going through a long, drawn-out trial."

Relief and anger washed over her. Anger that it had even happened at all, but at least that monster would be locked up, unable to hurt anyone else. "Really?"

"In exchange for going to the prison of his choice and a few other small things, he made things relatively easy." Georgina shrugged, looking as surprised as Evie felt.

"Thank you. For this, for everything."

"You just got me a promotion with this bust." Georgina didn't look thrilled, however. Probably because so many people had been killed because of Ben.

Standing, Evie held out a hand and shook Georgina's. "You know where to find me if you need anything."

"Just stay out of trouble."

"I plan on it." Hell, she planned on heading to the hospital to see her brother—who was supposed to be released soon—and then spending time with her family.

All while trying to not obsess over Dylan and how she'd lost the best thing that had ever happened to her.

CHAPTER TWENTY-TWO

E vie felt as if she was on autopilot as she walked down the hospital hallway toward the private waiting room. Her parents were with Evan right now since he'd finally allowed them to see him, so she was going to wait until they were done. Her mom had come over again last night, bringing food that Evie hadn't been able to eat and generally taking care of her as if she'd been a teenager crying over a broken heart. Which she'd never actually had as a teenager because she hadn't been interested in boys back then.

It had been two full days since she'd seen Dylan, and she didn't feel much better this morning but that didn't matter. Now that things with Ben were mostly wrapped up, she planned to spend as much time with her family as possible.

She'd called and texted Dylan again, hoping for some kind of response, but she'd gotten radio silence. Which was expected—even if it hurt.

When she stepped inside the waiting room she was surprised to find Isla leaning against the tinted window, staring out over the parking lot. Isla turned to look at her, her expression softening when she saw Evie. "Hey, are you okay? You look... That is to say..."

"I know I look like garbage. It's okay." She felt like it too. Her eyes were puffy from crying and she hadn't bothered with makeup. Or food. Or a shower. "Has anything changed with you and Evan?"

Isla's expression tightened, her eyes almost going cold. Evie knew what the other woman was doing—shutting down and protecting herself. "Evan still won't see me. I came by one last time to see if he'd change his mind. He hasn't. And I just need to deal with it. A lot of people are depending on me now that my father is..." Her voice broke slightly but she cleared her throat. "Gone. I guess I need to get on with my new life."

Evie stepped farther into the room and sat on one of the couches. She motioned for Isla to sit with her.

Wearing a forest green shift dress and looking incredibly elegant, Isla sat on the other end. She hadn't been staying here, thankfully. No, she'd finally started sleeping at home and taking care of herself. Though she looked as if she'd lost about ten pounds—ten pounds she couldn't afford to lose in the first place.

Despite the weight loss and exhaustion surrounding Isla, this was the put-together, sleek woman Evie remembered from before the bombing. "I'm so sorry about your dad. I know I've said it, but I really am. And I'm really, really sorry my brother is such an asshole."

Isla jerked back at Evie's bluntness and let out a sharp, sudden laugh. "You know what? I'm sorry he's being an asshole too. None of this makes sense to me but I'm done trying to figure him out."

"Good for you. I think he might come around." At least Evie hoped he did. Or her brother was going to regret letting Isla go, for the rest of his life.

Isla lifted a shoulder. "I don't think I care if he does. I'm done, Evie. Done and just tired."

Evie heard the lie for what it was but didn't respond. Instead she simply nodded. At least Isla would have closure about the bombing, about the man who'd killed her father and others. That was one silver lining for her and everyone else who had been hurt.

"Have you heard anything about Ellis?" Isla continued, leaning over to the glass and wood coffee table and picking up her purse, clearly ready to get out of there.

"No," she said, wishing she had news because it would mean there was progress.

"I have something I want to give to Evan. It's a letter and I know you're the only person who can make sure he gets it." Isla pulled a cream-colored envelope out of her purse and started to hand it to Evie, but paused. "Will I be putting you in a weird situation to do this?"

"Of course not." Going against her normal instincts, Evie took the letter then clasped Isla's hands in her own. "I swear, he will eventually pull his head out of his ass. And when he does, he's going to be sorry for all of this. And just because he's not talking to you doesn't mean I'm not here. And my parents too. If you need anything, please let me know. It's not a hollow offer. I know you'll be dealing with a lot with your dad's business. I'm doing contract work now so...just reach out."

Isla's eyes filled with tears but she quickly dashed them away before straightening. "This would be so much easier if you guys were sort of horrible," she murmured.

Evie let out a startled laugh. "What, like you want me to cut you out or start being mean to you?"

Laughing lightly, Isla shook her head. "No, definitely not. It's just...I feel so untethered right now. As if Evan has cut things between us but they're not quite really severed. His family, including you, are so wonderful. But it's like he doesn't exist, like he died when he really didn't. I understand he's dealing with a lot after the explosion, but him refusing to see me... It's hard to deal with. And you guys, his family, you've all been so wonderful when you're dealing with your own stuff, especially with Ellis. I feel like I'm losing my family."

Throat tight, Evie slid down the couch and pulled Isla into a tight hug. When she pulled back, she said, "I hope one day I get to call you my sister."

Isla blinked and cleared her throat. "I can't start crying again. I might not stop if I do."

Evie tucked the letter into her purse. "I'll make sure he gets this. And as soon as he's out of the hospital bed, I'm going to kick his ass for you."

Isla let out another rusty-sounding laugh as she stood. "I never know what's going to come out of your mouth."

Evie had started to respond when she heard the door behind her open. Turning, she froze to see Dylan standing there. She jerked to her feet but couldn't make herself talk. She just stood there, staring, her heart thudding in her ears.

Isla murmured a quick goodbye and slipped past Dylan as he stepped into the room.

Evie drank him in, memorizing every inch of him, watching as if she hadn't seen him in years as opposed to days. He had on casual slacks and a button-down shirt. With a couple days' worth of stubble and tired eyes, he looked sexy but about as bad as she felt. For some reason, that didn't make her feel better. She didn't want him to be suffering.

"Why are you here?" she blurted, finally finding her voice as she took a small step forward.

"To see you." He said the words as if they should be obvious.

She wasn't sure how he'd even known she was here, but her heart leapt. "I'm so sorry," she whispered, not sure what else to say. She wanted to get it tattooed on her. Because she was sorry. So very sorry. And she wasn't sure she could ever make things right.

Sighing, he rubbed a hand over his face as he moved into the room, giving her distance as he sat in one of the cushioned chairs.

She perched on the edge of the couch, all her muscles pulled bowstring tight as she watched him. It was good to see him but confusing. She wanted to go to him, to pull him into her arms and apologize again, beg him to give her another chance, but she knew that would be foolish. Maybe he was here to get closure. If so, she was going to do her best to give it to him. She owed him that much at least.

"I've had time to think about what happened. About what you did," he said.

She simply nodded, not sure what to say.

He rubbed a hand over his face again. "I know why you did what you did. I read about that takedown of Jensen and the human smuggling ring he was running through Miami. He was garbage and he deserved worse than what he got."

The man had been killed in prison, far too easy a death as far as Evie was concerned. But he was dead and gone, and there was some justice in that. "In the beginning, when I was learning about who you were, I fell for you a little bit then. For the record, that's never happened on a job before. And I didn't sleep with you to get an introduction," she said though she'd already told him virtually the same before. Now that he was sitting in front of her, she wanted to fully explain herself.

"Yeah, I know that. Samara came to see me."

Evie jerked back in surprise.

His mouth lifted into a smile. "She said you didn't know about her visit. I'd wondered if she was lying."

"I didn't know," she rushed out. "And I'm sorry—"

"You've apologized enough. I don't want you to keep doing it."

"What *do* you want?" It was too much to hope that he might forgive her, want to be with her. But she was hanging on to that tiny, pathetic shred of it.

Sighing, he stood and moved around the little coffee table and sat next to her on the couch. "Maybe I'm a fool but I still want you in my life. Still care for you. More than care for you."

Throat tight, she said, "I love you, Dylan. That was real—is real. I never faked anything with you... Except liking wine. I'm more of a beer kind of girl. But that was my only lie...other than who I worked for. And I won't lie to you ever again. You know who I am now, and if I can't tell you something, I'll just be honest about it."

His smile grew just the tiniest bit as he watched her, that familiar sexy look stealing over his expression.

Butterflies launched inside her at the sight of him softening. Could he really forgive her? Could they truly start fresh?

Reaching out, he took her hand in his. "I don't want any more lies between us."

"Can you forgive me?" she asked, even though he'd said he understood her reasoning. "Because I don't want conditional forgiveness where I feel guilty for the rest of..." She wanted to say "for the rest of our lives" but that sounded ridiculous. He wasn't really offering her a future even if she wanted one with him. He was here wanting answers from her. Answers he deserved.

"I forgive you. I understand why you did what you did. My ego is hurt that you targeted me when I fell hard for you the moment I met you."

Her throat thickened. "I fell for you at the cocktail party too. We might have targeted you, but the attraction between us, that was real. My feelings, those are real."

He gave her a long look. "You swear you didn't sleep with me as part of the job?"

"I swear. I had already gotten the introduction to Jensen. I'm not sure if you even remember, but I had.

And I was supposed to end things with you later that night."

"I do remember." He watched her carefully, his eyes searching hers.

She swallowed. "So where do we go from here?"

Dylan sighed. "How about I grab us lunch and then we go see your brother? And then...come home with me."

She blinked in surprise, hope soaring inside her. "Really?"

He nodded, reaching up and cupping her cheek gently. "Really. I want to start over with you, build a life with you. I'm not walking away, Evie. The last two days without you have shown me that. And I'm not going to hold this over your head. My forgiveness is not conditional." Tears sprang to her eyes, but he gently wiped her cheeks with his thumbs. "Don't cry," he murmured, leaning forward to kiss her. "I don't like your tears."

She leaned into the kiss, pressing her mouth to his and clinging to him as if she was afraid he would change his mind and run out the door. Evie couldn't believe he was here, that he'd forgiven her. It had been too much to hope.

But here he was, Dylan Blackwood in the flesh, kissing her senseless. She just hoped this was real, that she wasn't dreaming. That she wasn't going to wake up soon and find out she'd imagined everything.

* * *

"Do you need to stop by your brother's place to get the rest of your stuff?" Dylan asked as he pulled out of the hospital parking lot an hour later. Evie had taken a cab here so he was taking her back where she belonged. His house. And he wasn't letting her go again.

She looked at him in surprise. "What do you mean?"

He was still reeling after everything he'd learned about her, but he knew one thing: he wasn't letting her out of his life again. "I mean, how much stuff do you have left over there? If it's a lot I can have someone move it to my place." He felt her gaze on him as he pulled up to a stoplight. "What?"

"What are you even saying?" Her voice was tentative, very un-Evie.

"Pretty sure my meaning is crystal clear." He'd forgiven her and he had been honest with her. He wasn't going to hold this over her head. That was no way to start this relationship over. He truly understood why she'd done what she'd done, even if he hated that he'd been a pawn. But she'd proven herself to be an incredibly strong woman at her core, going above and beyond to help others.

Yes, his ego was hurt that she'd targeted him and that he'd been such an easy mark. But the chemistry between them was undeniable. His feelings for her were true. As she put it, he'd seen both versions of her and he loved all of her. Every single layer. The last week had proven that. He'd gotten to see the real Evie in action and he loved every bit of her. He couldn't walk away from her, from them.

"You want me to move in with you?" she whispered.

"You *are* moving in with me."

She lifted an eyebrow. "Are you ordering me?"

"No. I'm simply stating a fact. You don't have a home and I do. And I'm not going to spend one night away from you. I plan to go to bed with you every evening and wake up to your face every morning." He was all in. And this was how he'd always done things. When he wanted something, he went for it. Now was no different.

She stared at him in surprise, her cheeks flushing pink. She cleared her throat. "I actually do have some things over there that I'd like to get. I can grab them tomorrow though."

Good. He wanted to get her back to his place so he could bury himself inside her for hours. Sleeping without her for even one night had been torture. It had given him a lot of time alone with his thoughts, which ended up being a good thing. Life without her was torture—she was *his*.

His mother had always told him that when he met the woman who was meant to be his, he would know, and he did.

He and Evie Bishop belonged together.

CHAPTER TWENTY-THREE

Evie zipped up her suitcase and tugged it off the guest bed. It felt a little weird to be leaving her brother's house, but not weird to be going to Dylan's house. Because that was exactly where she belonged.

After they'd returned to his place last night they hadn't been able to keep their hands off each other. The only reason she'd even left the house this morning was to meet with the FBI again for another wrap-up meeting, to go see Samara, who was staying in a condo now—and apparently dating Finn—and then Dylan had brought her here to grab her final belongings.

"Evie! You need to get down here." There was a weird note in Dylan's voice, making her leave her suitcase right where it was and pull out her weapon. Moving silently, she hurried down the stairs, pistol out.

When she reached the bottom stair, she froze for all of a second when she saw who was standing with her brother in the living room. She quickly tucked her weapon away. Dylan stepped back, giving them a little privacy, but didn't leave the room. He knew exactly who her brother was so she didn't need to introduce them.

"Ellis!" She rushed at him, wrapping her arms around him in a tackle hug. He was a lot taller than her—she was the only Bishop who hadn't gotten all the height—so she was practically hanging on to him but she didn't care. He was here. He was alive.

He squeezed back tight. "Little sister," he rasped out. "I didn't think you'd be here."

When she stepped back, she realized she had tears on her cheeks so she quickly swept them away. "Where have you been?" She punched him in the shoulder for good measure. He had a beard now and he'd definitely lost weight, but he hadn't lost his edge. She could see the steely determination in his blue eyes.

"Weak, Evie," he murmured, even as his expression hardened. "I've been set up."

"Yeah, no joke. We all know that. We've got an attorney on retainer ready to represent you. Just come in. We'll make this better."

He simply lifted an eyebrow. "That's not going to happen. If I come in, I'll be killed almost immediately."

Fear for him grabbed her. "I have contacts in the FBI. And I'm sure you do too. They'll help keep you protected. You'll be treated—"

"No," he snapped out. Then he softened his tone and continued, "I've got this. Just trust me. I'm working on something to clear my name. It's all going to be okay. This is just something I have to do."

She wanted to argue with him but held her tongue. Instead she nodded. "Mom and Dad are worried about you. So is Evan."

He closed his eyes for a moment, his jaw tightening. "How is Evan?"

"He was just released from the hospital. We're going over there tonight to see him. He's...not doing good though. Even if he tries to pretend that he is. Physically he'll be fine, I'm just worried about his emotional state." She'd never seen Evan like this before—depressed and withdrawn.

"At least he has Isla."

Evie shook her head. "He won't see her, wouldn't let her into the hospital room. He's being a real dick."

Ellis looked surprised but quickly shook his head. "Look, I can't stay long. I just stopped by to grab something."

"The Feds have combed over this place. And so have a couple guys who were killed in DEA custody." She started to tell him all about it but he shook his head.

"I know. They didn't get what I came for, trust me." His expression was grim.

She wanted him to stay but didn't want to risk him being caught because of her stubbornness. For all she knew the Feds were still watching the house. Though she kinda doubted it since no one had stormed the place. Whatever he'd come for, it must be important for him to risk it in the middle of the day. "Fine. But you have my number. Call me. I can help."

"I promise I'll stay in touch. I'm going to fix this. There's an endgame to all this bullshit and I'm not going to lose."

Lunging forward again, she wrapped him in a tight hug. "If for some reason you can't, I'll help you get out of the country. I'll help you get set up somewhere else under a new ID."

"I'll help too," Dylan said, the first words he'd spoken since she'd come downstairs. "I've got properties around the world."

Ellis gave her a soft smile, then looked at Dylan. "I don't think it will come to that. I'm going to get my life back. Count on it. Blackwood, take care of my sister."

"We'll take care of each other."

Ellis nodded, half-smiling. "Good answer."

Though Evie didn't want to go, she let Dylan grab her suitcase from upstairs and hurried out with him.

"I hate leaving him," she said to Dylan once they were in his car, heading down the quiet residential street.

"I'll do everything in my power to make sure that he has help."

She simply nodded, unsure what else to say. Leaving Ellis back there went against every instinct inside her.

"I gave him some addresses of a few properties I own that aren't being used. If he needs safe houses, he's got them."

Surprised, she turned away from looking out the window to face him. "Are you serious?"

"Yes. He showed up while you were packing and we talked for a few minutes."

"Dylan...if he gets caught, you could be in trouble for harboring a fugitive."

Dylan shrugged. "I'm not worried. Besides, he's your family, so that means he's mine too."

Throat tight, she managed to rasp out a "Thank you" even though it wasn't nearly enough. Reaching over, she squeezed his hand in hers. She wasn't ever letting this man go.

CHAPTER TWENTY-FOUR

Evie glanced up from the patio table when Leo stepped outside. She frowned at the sight of him. He wasn't supposed to be working today—which was part of the reason she'd set this up today. Over the last week with Dylan, she'd come to the decision. He had forgiven her, yes, but he'd also put himself out there for her and her family. He'd made himself vulnerable before and she'd hurt him badly.

It didn't matter that she hadn't wanted to. Even though she knew they weren't keeping score, she needed to be vulnerable in front of him, to be bold. And if this backfired, then... She was pretty sure she deserved the rejection, if so.

"This is a nice spread." Leo's tone was neutral. He'd been perfectly polite since she'd moved into Dylan's place. Polite and reserved and nothing like the man she'd gotten to know before over the months she'd basically lived here.

She simply nodded and straightened the tablecloth. Then she moved over to the stepladder and climbed up it, positioning the twinkle lights. Cooper stood next to the ladder, his tail wagging as he watched her with a curious expression. He'd been her little helper—or more likely hoping to sneak any food if it fell off the table.

She'd learned that he was a shameless beggar when it came to treats.

"Want some help?" Leo asked.

"Seriously?"

He shrugged and slid his jacket off, tossing it onto one of the chairs. Then he grabbed the other ladder leaning against one of the columns. He moved it to the opposite side of the patio and tightened the entire string so it wasn't sagging.

"So what's going on here tonight?" His tone was casual, but she didn't believe it.

"Just dinner."

He snorted, his dark eyes knowing. "Yeah, right."

She shot him a sharp look, then sighed. "Look, I'm sorry I lied to you."

"Are you?"

"I did what I had to do." She stepped off the ladder then looked around at her handiwork. She would never be a designer but she thought the whole spread looked pretty good—Champagne, strawberries, cheeses and all sorts of other stuff that her mom had actually picked out. She wanted to do this right and had confessed her plan to her—and her mom had been more than happy to get all the little details right.

"I don't know all the specifics. But I know that Dylan is happy to have you back in his life."

"I'm happy to be here. More than happy. And I'm not going anywhere." She shot him a challenging stare.

His mouth kicked up in a half-grin. "Good. I always liked you two together."

She raised an eyebrow.

"What? I *always* liked you, Evie. I knew you loved him and weren't after his money. But you broke his heart."

"Yeah, I know. It was the last thing I wanted to do."

"I know that now. By the way, I've been wanting to ask you... When I helped you with target practice..." He let the unspoken question hang in the air.

She inwardly winced. "I'm an expert shot. I just couldn't let you know then."

"We'll see how expert you are. Next week, me and you at the range. A competition. Loser buys the winner a beer."

"You're on." She knew she'd been officially forgiven by Leo too and that mattered. Because he mattered to Dylan. And she really liked the guy.

Leo cleared his throat as he stepped back to the patio doors. "Fair warning. His schedule changed. He'll be home in twenty minutes."

She jerked to attention. "Seriously? You couldn't tell me that before?" She hadn't even showered yet.

He simply grinned at her and headed back inside.

Evie followed, Cooper hot on her heels as she headed in the direction of Dylan's bedroom. No, *their* bedroom. It was most definitely theirs now, something he kept reminding her of. Which was weird to say. She'd always traveled so much that she'd never considered her small condo in DC a home. Not a real one anyway. It had been a place she laid her head at night when she was in the country.

Luckily she was used to getting ready fast, so after a short shower and quickly running a blow dryer through her hair, she slid on a slinky little red dress with nothing underneath.

Then she grabbed the little box she'd been hiding in her nightstand and hurried to the patio, calling Dylan as she walked through the maze of hallways. "Where are you?" she asked when he picked up.

"Just got home. Pulling into the drive now."

"Meet me on the patio." She ended the call before he could say anything else, nerves punching through her.

Feeling ridiculously edgy, she sat down at the table. Then she stood, feeling silly for sitting. Cooper watched her curiously again, clearly confused with what she was doing. How was she going to do this? Hell, *should* she even do this? It was probably too soon.

Her instinct told her it wasn't. Not for them. But...maybe she was wrong and projecting her own feelings. Maybe this wasn't what he wanted at all now.

She'd been trying to think of a way to show Dylan that she was all in. When he'd proposed to her, it had shifted her entire world on its axis. She hadn't been expecting it. At all. Looking back, she probably should have.

And the thing was, when he had proposed she'd wanted to say yes. Desperately so. But if she had, it would've been based on a big lie. So she'd said no and then run.

"What's all this?" Dylan asked, stepping outside to join her, a tired smile on his face as he leaned down to pet Cooper. He'd been working on a huge project the last couple days and something told her he'd put it off the week before because of the insanity of her life.

She hadn't accepted any offers for contract work so she'd had plenty of time with her thoughts, plenty of time to know exactly what she had to do. Wanted to do.

She stepped forward, sweat beading at the base of her spine. Damn, how did men work up the courage to do this? "I love you, Dylan." Evie loved the way his expression subtly lit up whenever she said the words. So she said them as often as possible now.

"Yeah, I know," he murmured, grinning as he stepped around the table, pulling her into his arms.

"I want to spend my life with you," she continued, working up the courage to completely and utterly put herself out there. She clutched the jewelry box in her hand, trying to get the right words out. She pulled it out and started to open it, but to her surprise, he went down on one knee and pulled out the same jewelry box he'd proposed with before.

She stared at him.

"I love you and want to spend my life with you too, Evie Bishop. And you are *not* proposing to me." He took the little box from her hand and set it aside—she'd bought him a simple wedding band she still hoped he wanted to wear. Then he opened the red box and that same gorgeous ring from before was there nestled inside, sparkling under the lights. "I'm traditional on some things."

"Dylan," she whispered.

"Marry me?" His expression was full of love.

"Yes." She wrapped her arms around him, practically tackling him to the ground.

Cooper barked as if in agreement before heading back inside.

Laughing, Dylan stood, scooping her into his arms as he sat at the table. As she settled into his lap, he said, "Unless you want it, I don't want a big wedding."

She shook her head. "Hell no. We can do a courthouse wedding. Or something simple here. I don't care about stuff like that." Never had. Hell, she'd never even thought of getting married until he came along.

"As soon as we can get a license, we'll do something quiet."

She hated that Ellis wouldn't be there but she nodded and leaned closer, brushing her lips over Dylan's.

He deepened the kiss for a long moment before pulling back. "There's only one guard at the gate tonight and a couple patrolling the front. They have strict orders not to come around back. And I sent everyone else home." Heat flared in his eyes.

She shifted on his lap, straddling him. "Did you know that I was going to do this?"

"No. But Leo told me it would probably be a good idea if I sent everyone home," he said, grinning.

So Leo really had forgiven her. Evie laughed lightly. "Wise man."

"This week, Evie. I'm not waiting any longer. I know your family situation is less than ideal, but I want you as my wife."

Throat tight, she nodded. "And I want you as my husband."

Something like relief flickered across his features, as if he'd expected her to push back, before he crushed his mouth to hers. She sank into his embrace and kiss, savoring every second of it as they held on to each other.

So much was still up in the air for her family. Evan was out of the hospital, but not the man he'd been before the explosion. And Ellis was still in hiding, wanted for murder.

But she would help both her brothers. Her whole family.

And she was going to do it with the man she loved by her side.

Thank you for reading Bishop's Knight. I'm excited to bring you a new trilogy and I hope you've enjoyed the first book. If you'd like to stay in touch with me and be the first to learn about new releases, sign up for my newsletter at https://katiereus.com

ACKNOWLEDGMENTS

I owe a lot of gratitude to Kaylea Cross for helping me plot out this first book in a new trilogy. Getting the first book right is so important and I'm grateful for those brainstorming sessions. For my assistant, Sarah, thank you for all you do to keep things running smoothly. For Julia, thank you for your thorough edits. Jaycee, thank you for another amazing cover. To my wonderful readers, thank you for taking this new journey with me! For my family, thank you for your continuing support. And to God, I have abounding gratitude.

COMPLETE BOOKLIST

Darkness Series
Darkness Awakened
Taste of Darkness
Beyond the Darkness
Hunted by Darkness
Into the Darkness
Saved by Darkness
Guardian of Darkness
Sentinel of Darkness
A Very Dragon Christmas
Darkness Rising

Deadly Ops Series
Targeted
Bound to Danger
Chasing Danger (novella)
Shattered Duty
Edge of Danger
A Covert Affair

Endgame Trilogy
Bishop's Knight
Bishop's Queen
Bishop's Endgame

ABOUT THE AUTHOR

Katie Reus is the *New York Times* and *USA Today* bestselling author of the Red Stone Security series, the Darkness series and the Deadly Ops series. She fell in love with romance at a young age thanks to books she pilfered from her mom's stash. Years later she loves reading romance almost as much as she loves writing it.

However, she didn't always know she wanted to be a writer. After changing majors many times, she finally graduated summa cum laude with a degree in psychology. Not long after that she discovered a new love. Writing. She now spends her days writing dark paranormal romance and sexy romantic suspense.

For more information on Katie please visit her website: https://katiereus.com